Madala, an aging wife-beating, racist Afrikaner policeman, and make you empathize with him while simultaneously loathing him is an incredible feat of literary imagination. She makes you want to take the journey down his heart of darkness, to understand why and how he became the monster he is so ashamed of being.

Futhi's characterization of an array of resilient women from different eras in South African history paints us a picture of the true backbone of our country—women who not only nurture and sustain families, but have the courage to carve new paths by breaking the shackles of both stereotype and social pressure. This novel turns the lights on while darkness envelops us."
—HEATHER ROBERTSON, editor of *Daily Maverick 168*

"Built around tightly-knit nuggets of first-person accounts that fit into one another like puzzle pieces, reading this novel is like standing naked beneath a waterfall during an African summer. Ntshingila uses an amazing repertoire of storytelling techniques to peel layer after layer of the human side of the South African tragedy, often referenced glibly when we write and speak of, 'the Apartheid era,' 'the struggle,' 'the Blacks,' the whites' or 'the new South Africa.' The reader of this book will be plunged deep into the bowels of South Africa's dark past. But the reader will also be led towards a brilliant and bright day that beckons. In the process, the reader will be educated, shaken and entertained. In this novel, Ntshingila achieves what every Truth Commission attempts, namely to shed light on the past, truthfully, passionately and compassionately."
—TINYIKO MALULEKE, senior research fellow, University of Pretoria Centre for the Advancement of Scholarship

THEY GOT TO YOU TOO

A NOVEL BY

FUTHI NTSHINGILA

Interlink Books

An imprint of Interlink Publishing Group, Inc.
Northampton, Massachusetts

First American edition published in 2023 by

Interlink Books
An imprint of Interlink Publishing Group, Inc.
46 Crosby Street, Northampton, MA 01060
www.interlinkbooks.com

First published in South Africa in 2021 by Pan Macmillan South Africa

ISBN-13: 978-1-62371-741-4

Library of Congress Control Number: 2023941535
LC record available at: https://lccn.loc.gov/2023941535

Printed and bound in the United States of America

This is for my father, Bernard Mtwanas Ntshingila,
the gentle giant.

*"The act of writing was too personally important for me
to abandon it just because the prospects of my being
taken seriously were bleak."*—Toni Morrison

I heard all of you, thank you for trusting me with your stories.

MADALA

IF I AM BEING honest, before I ended up here as a heap of troublesome old bones, I will say that my body did give me enough warning that something was amiss. I repeatedly ignored the signs. I was well adjusted to discomfort and my pa had always told me to toughen up. He hated any display of weakness and I suppose as much as I had sworn never to be like him I was turning into him. Isn't that how it works? We wake up one day having turned into exactly what we have been attempting to outrun. We look in a mirror and horror hits us with the inevitability. I felt it; I had morphed into my father. A slimy feeling washed up from my gut and burned my throat, making me gag.

But I digress. My warning was not audible, it was corporeal and started with a tiny, almost imperceptible, prodding. I liken it to when you've had those jabs for malaria and drunk numerous cans of tonic water. You get that slightly unpleasant but manageable and even ignorable ill feeling—a woozy head rush and clammy hands. My ears were constantly ringing but I ignored it. Next, I would wake up with pins and needles in my feet but after some movement and a shower I would be as right as rain again. My body ramped up the warning from a murmur to an audible "help" that I could not ignore but I had to endure. It was the voices and tormenting laughs that had me in the fetal position, frozen with fear. I would grit my teeth and hang on for the signs of dawn to come and save me. I was pathetic; a fully grown man past andropause with fully visible man-boobs and nuts so droopy that even cold water did not manage to lift them up, yet here I was afraid of the dark.

Even if I could have done something, what would I do? Go to the doctor and say what? I hear the voices of the men I killed in the army all those years ago. No, there is just too much riding on this after keeping my head down for so long and all that TRC dirty linen and other witch-hunt missions that I had managed to escape. Now I must go to a doctor? Who is to say where it will end up? I can just see the headline about another evil dinosaur that got off from killing and torturing Blacks has come out of the woodwork. My demons might as well take a Michael Jackson grotesque Thriller walk and come and drag me to my grave.

I am an ex-police officer, one of the few who braved the new dispensation and found it bearable enough, even enjoyable, to be part of. I successfully reinvented myself as Joshua Doore, the friendly uncle who mentored some of the youngsters in the force. I needed it more than they did,

I think. I cashed out my pension in 2004 already but they kept me on to advise; an "institutional memory" is what they called me. What was I going to do sitting at home anyway, wifeless and childless? I felt obliged to stay and earn a healthy and steady income and invest my nest-egg pension. One day when I am dead I will finally make good on my son. I don't want to speculate on whether he would even acknowledge me and my money. Maybe he will give it all to charity or burn it; who knows. It hurts me to think of my son, so I don't.

I am rewriting the wrongs I committed on my son and wife by becoming a kind uncle to young, mostly Black, rookies that I used to eat for breakfast in my heyday. Once in a while we would get an intake of a handful of white kids joining the force but it was becoming more and more rare. I have come to forge relationships with some of these kids that sometimes bring tears to my eyes. I will go to my grave never having told them what I did in the Zimbabwean veld and Mozambican trenches.

First thing I did during the mayhem of the sunset clause was to transfer from Natal to Pretoria, putting distance between me and my old haunts. Ironically, if I really think about it, I was getting back to where it all started, where my father's dry white bones are resting, if that's even possible. So I am careful with my stories. I don't drink, it loosens the tongue and I don't miss it. I have saved a lot of money since dropping that liquid demon. In my day I would become aggressive, break things, fight people and brandish guns; the worst kind of fool is what I was back then.

"Madala" is what the rookies call me; it's affectionate.

I'll give it to these kids, first they give you a tough time and push you as hard as they can but once they begin to trust you, you become like family. So I really liked it when I found out that I am known as "Madala" in their informal circles. Sometimes when we were all relaxing they would forget the stiff formalities and call me "Madala." Some climbed the ranks and when they bumped into me I was a madala who taught them to stiffen their spine. Not all rookies liked me; some were resentful and as far as they were concerned I didn't belong in the academy. I never did let on that I could understand isiZulu and I could cuss them out better than some of these kids who dreamed and thought in English. In fact, for some years growing up, I had to think in isiZulu and translate into Afrikaans. It's funny how the worm turns.

I would sit with my office window open and listen to them test their political ideas. One rookie, whose eyes always seemed to bore into my soul, was holding court outside my window talking about the foolishness of leadership for preserving old fogies like me in the academy.

"Hayi bafwethu, this thing is not only wrong, it is downright dangerous. My grandfather once told me an old cautionary tale of a frozen snake. A man happens upon a small frozen mamba; he takes it home and leaves it by the warm hearth when he goes to bed. The snake thaws and slithers to where the man sleeps, bites the man's ankle, unloading its venom. It glides away, leaving him cold, frozen and, later, six feet under. This is what the academy is doing, taking a frozen mamba from the old order. Who knows? He could be briefing his compatriots on all our secrets and one day we won't wake up from our sleep."

"Heee haaa uqalile, Sam; here you go again. Madala is one of us, mfana. He is fair to the bone. In fact, sometimes I think that old man gives the Boers a harder time than us. Have you seen how he corrected the new rookies who were becoming overfamiliar with him? Isn't he the one who ratted on old Van Wyk when he called Suzy a kaffir bitch? Man, that cracker of a slap he landed on Van Wyk sobered him up one time!" The boys laugh, remembering the commotion that day in the academy.

"You're right, Madala is one of a kind. His swift justice delivery gave me a new kind of respect for him. He's not like the others and they don't like him one bit. I heard them say he brown-noses too much with the unwashed masses. That's what they secretly call the Black generals and the commissioner," said the other rookie, dismissing Sam's suspicions.

It was amusing listening to the rookies and satisfying to know I have earned their trust. They're right, I did slap the shit out of Van Wyk. It was almost like an automatic reflex. He was new and cocky and, having seen that the principal of the academy is a Boer like him, he thought he could get away with things. He groped the wrong girl; a rookie who turned around and rained solid punches to his gut. She finished him with a mother of a kick to his nuts. That's when he resorted to the insults he must have heard growing up. "Kaffir bitch," he spat out. I witnessed all of it and I was walking behind him after practice. I was onto him like lightning. I never said a word. Van Wyk and everyone watching were hushed to silence by the speed, intensity and shock of the slap I delivered.

It activated something in me that had lain dormant. I was shaking with something deeper than anger as I marched to my quarters. I longed for a long drag of something stronger than a cigarette. I needed a joint. I lay down and found myself thinking back to when I was a young boy, my small hand in Kristina's sandpaper-rough hand walking to the ice-cream truck. It was a hot day, so hot that I was turning red and Kristina was sweating. The truck driver refused to sell her ice-cream so she took me aside, gave me the money and instructed me to stand on my toes and buy my own ice-cream. I couldn't buy two because the man said he didn't do business with a "kaffir bitch." It was the meanest thing I had ever heard and remained bitter in my gut for a long time.

Kristina said the man was mean because he was afraid and she told me not to repeat the incident to my Oumagrootjie. I didn't but I also lost all pleasure eating that ice-cream. We shared it. Kristina and I played a game of licking the ice-cream in turns until she let me have the cone. The man saw us sharing the ice-cream, swiftly stopped the truck and ran over to us. He slapped Kristina so hard in the face I thought she was going to fall but she just held her face, looked him in the eye and laughed so hard.

"How does it feel being powerful? I know you and your mother. You can pass all you want, you will never be white."

Kristina's words were like an air-sucking punch. I saw the man recoil and speed walk back to his truck.

"Yes, run and send my love to Betty September," shouted Kristina. "Your mother Beatrice. That's right, that was her name before she was Betty September. I know your dirty little secret. What's the matter Big Baas? Did I hurt your feelings?"

Kristina was taunting the man and he screeched away in the ice-cream truck and switched off the singsong lullaby. Kristina stood watching him and laughed dementedly.

$$\equiv$$

I woke up with a start, drenched in sweat, and I could just make out the sound of Kristina's frightening laughter fading into the ether. It was so real and frightening that I decided then and there that I was getting too old for any of this. I needed to convince the commissioner to let me go and live out my old age with my peers. I was told to wait until the rookies were drill-ready for the 2019 inauguration, which meant that by the end of 2018 the rookies would be ready and waiting. I could start the new year as a proper old man living in an old-age home. It was both frightening and liberating at the same time.

I tried to hang on but my body was done. On long drill days, my stubborn streak began to humiliate me in front of the rookies and the seniors I was overseeing. I fainted, along with some of those young ones, because of the heat. I began to lose words. In my head I was clear and I knew what I wanted to say but my mind and my mouth were not connected. I became a mumbling mess and would point to things to make sense of something; sometimes I'd grab at things out of frustration. The farewell they planned for me is a blur in my memory, with the exception of a large picture frame that had photos of me with all the presidents, from President Nelson Mandela to President Ramaphosa. It was my treasured pride and joy.

Looking at those photos I could see a physical deterioration of how my body was slowly giving in. In the photo with President Nelson Mandela I was steady, standing straight but already greying at 55. Still cocky and defiant but maybe a little unsure of my fate with the new dispensation. I remember before he became president when they put me in a security detail that accompanied him to his visit to Cuba. We advanced, getting there two weeks before him to liaise with the Cuban security team, planning routes and making sure nothing could harm our soon-to-be commander-in-chief.

Those were heady times for me, visiting a communist country of men and women who fought us tooth and nail in those trenches of the border wars. I was calm on the outside but jumpy as shit inside. The old women, dressed in all white, were still following the old African religion of the slaves who ended up there. I didn't like their stares and there was one with a large cigar permanently hanging out the side of her mouth. She heard we were from South Africa and while most of the Cubans we met were happy to see us and automatically exclaimed, "Ah Si Mandela, Hasta La Victoria Siempre," she demanded to know if we had seen her son. Our translator told us that she never stopped mourning the loss of her Pedro, the son who went to fight the war in Africa and never came back. It was uncomfortable looking in the eyes of a woman whose son I might have shot and whose thrashing body I might have jumped over during the war. Then she came straight at me, a short little woman, who stretched out her hands and pulled my face down to her level and kissed my forehead, just like Kristina did all those years ago. My heart was so full that day I cried myself to sleep.

In the photograph taken with President Mbeki, I look like a man who was sure-footed, having established myself as a reference point. Some people had even started calling me "Comrade Madala." I don't know how it came about but I embraced it. I sometimes had it so good that I had moments when I forgot the past.

If I look closer I can see that my back was starting to stoop a little in my mid-60s. I am decidedly weathered in the photo with President Motlanthe. We had gone through some tough times by then and I was feeling strained but I was still hanging on. I was a proper madala by the time they took the photo with President Zuma but still proud to serve. The photo with President Ramaphosa was taken at the State of the Nation address in 2018 after fierce negotiations with President Zuma. Alas, I was no longer serving by the time President Ramaphosa was inaugurated as president.

They did send a driver for me to attend the inauguration and I wore my full police regalia. I felt that I had to have done something right in my past life to have mistreated these people so badly during apartheid but still continue to be treated as a VIP in the time of them running the country. Some days I think it was actually my punishment because I never could relax, especially when they called me Comrade Madala.

Their warmth tore me apart because it buried my secrets deeper; they could never find out who I really was.

So I found myself here at De Groenkloof Old Age Home earlier than anticipated. I came in on one of my clear days and was as dignified and as gentlemanly as I could be. Ms. Rajah, the head of the home, was welcoming and understanding. I wrote down all my afflictions and apologized in advance for the fitful episodes I sometimes experienced. She read my notes carefully while I sat quietly and drank the tea I was served.

I have nothing to complain about with my living quarters. They are spacious and the view from my sunroom window is onto an over-manicured greenery that calms me. The doctor said he will monitor me but couldn't actually diagnose me with a specific condition.

The doctor is a young Black man with a wicked sense of humor, which immediately put me at ease. "Old Timer, you are just old and tired. Your brain scan doesn't show anything for me to be concerned about. There are no irregularities and you are in good shape for your age. If you were Black, Old Timer, I would say you are showing classic signs of being visited by the ones who have passed."

He laughed but I felt a cold dread passing through my body and settling in my gut like a localized anxiety. I smiled weakly but I felt ill. He picked up on my discomfort and the look of concern on his face made it even worse.

"Hey, I'm joking Old Timer, I didn't mean to frighten you. It's possible you are just adjusting to retirement. They worked you to the bone; you should have been traveling the world before it came to this."

He is nervous and doesn't know how to comfort an old man. I suddenly have an urge to put down the baggage of my nastiness of the past. Maybe it will silence the voices and my demons will know I have come clean, but how?

"That's alright, son. I'm just relieved that nothing is growing in my brain. I have abused this old body with all manner of unmentionables, including Mary Jane, as you youngsters call it. I'll be fine. Thank you, son."

He's not convinced but he plays along. "Sure Old Timer, and try to eat your vegetables. They have the best meals in this place; I want to come here when I retire! I'll monitor your situation closely but trust me, you're in good hands."

He leaves and I am left feeling relieved that there is nothing they could physically pick up, but it almost feels like that eerie silence before a devastating storm. I feel it in my bones.

$$\equiv$$

My first week in my new home I sleep peacefully. My dreams are vivid and of the past, taking me back to my time with Kristina. In one of the dreams, the two women who raised me—Kristina, and my great-grandmother, Oumagrootjie—are with me and we are happy, laughing together, while Oumagrootjie is drawing. I suddenly recall that before her death, Oumagrootjie had insomnia and anxiety like me and by the end she no longer spoke. I remember her journals and this memory comforts me some. It must be in the family to lose speech and words before death. I am dying. I have made peace with that, but what I am battling with is should I go to my grave with unconfessed confessions and shouldn't I be looking for my son so that I can apologize to him? I doubt his mother is still living and at this point I have no way of knowing.

I do the next best thing, like my Oumagrootjie used to do. I write things down. For a while everything seems to make sense and I feel a bit more settled. The trouble begins when my memory takes me back to the ugly days of the killings, the war and of me denouncing Kristina and betraying my family. The night nurses find themselves at their wits' end with me. I am swearing and swinging my weak fists at them. I wake up in the middle of the day feeling exhausted having only fallen asleep in the small hours. No one looks me in the eye and I overhear the staff say that there is no excuse for the language I use when I am having one of my fits, even if it is due to illness.

I recoil, I avoid the common room and I start to feel unsafe taking the walks in the garden. I am ashamed, like a sobered-up drunk the morning after. Ms. Rajah visits me to find out if there is anything she can do but I can't meet her eyes. She gives me herbal teas to try and help me calm down. During the day things subside. I'm not shouting or grunting aggressively at anyone. I don't mean to cause trouble but I am frustrated and frightened because I am losing the tools to be me. I feel betrayed by my mind.

It's like that time in my mid-40s, a time that most men know well, when my mind wanted to be a man but my body didn't come to attention. I remember that I was just as frightened then and convinced that God was punishing me for all the mess I had caused with all the women and the lies I had used to dodge my wife's questions. When a man comes face-to-face with mortality, he battles. I suppose my default is rage but this time, I must admit, my mind is already surrendering. I am fooling no one. I feel myself going down the drain. I fear the unknown.

≡

I've been in the home for a while but I'm not coping. Not having a routine like the one I had stuck to for decades has thrown me for a loop. I have declined rapidly and I am told a new night nurse is being dedicated to my care. I know what they are doing. They want her to leave as soon as she earns her first salary; she will not cope with me. I am known to be a nightmare to caregivers. I have dark episodes when I black out and launch into attacks, swearing like a demented sailor. I can't fall asleep so I sing or cry out through the night. I have long stopped drinking or smoking but when I turn it's like I have downed a whole bottle of Russian vodka. I'm ashamed of these episodes but I have no control over them. They have never brought in an outsider and I think I am a tolerated bemusement around here because if they let me go, where would I go? I have no one. I know that they know that I wouldn't last a day and so I use that to my advantage to prick at their conscience.

"You'd really do that to an 80-year-old man, huh? I could be your father. You wouldn't put your own father out to pasture just because he is a little, well, a little volatile, would you? Oh come now, you'll miss me when I finally croak."

I cock my head sideways and pull a puppy face. I shudder to think what I must be looking like trying to be cute. But it works, until I get into trouble again. If Ms. Rajah was white I would say she was a bleeding liberal. She's a softie who tries very hard to be tough but she doesn't fool me. I know very well that in her culture they never throw their elders into homes for the elderly. She thaws pretty quickly whenever I find myself in her office for something I have done. Our squabbles are like that of a daughter and an elderly father. I hate disappointing her but I know always that I will be forgiven because, well, she has never told me this but I know she is fond of me. She's never said it but I feel it, I know it. It feels familiar and warm even when I face a stern telling-off in her office.

Ms. Rajah comes from Goa, a beautiful part of India I once visited with a hippie who appeased my mid-life crisis at the time. Ms. Rajah has a dedication to help us old timers exit this world with dignity. A little scratch beneath the surface tells me someone elderly and dear to her died tragically and she, almost subconsciously, committed herself to prevent it from happening to other elders.

I am no shrink but Kristina taught me early on that there is a way to find things out about those around us without them even knowing. In my youth I dismissed it as hokey-pokey but there's something about getting old that you just know what you know without hankering after logical explanations. I no longer fear madness so being illogical does not threaten to undo my sanity. Anyway, it also occurred to me that Ms. Rajah brings out the boyishness in me. I feel like I can act a bit silly around her and not be judged harshly. It is rare to find such maternal warmth these days. Men have messed women up so badly that they no longer take any crap from anybody, especially an entitled old fart like me. So when I am given a cosmic chance to once again suckle at the benevolence of maternal care, I take it with gusto. I am not stupid, I know there are limits, so I play within those unwritten lines and boundaries.

This place is really not too bad. I am around plenty of other old timers and people my own age so I'm never lonely. My two sore points are that I cannot sleep and that I never have visitors. Nearly everyone has their adult children, grandchildren and friends come over for Saturday or Sunday dinner. It drives a knife through my heart and I become rotten to the nurses. I mean really rotten and I know it.

Most maddening are the scalding tears that defeat me. Oh hell, I can tell you that the punishment for our wrongdoing is right here on this earth, not with some two-horned red-eyed devil of eternal hell. No, it is right on this earth! I don't know how else to deal with my regrets. I have a son who must be married with children of his own by now. I don't blame him for cutting me out of his life. I gave him hell growing up. I didn't know any better; I was put through hell by my father so it's all I knew. It is a chapter of my life I choose to shelve into my failing memory. For an old man with many secrets to keep, it's easy to forget. It feels better not to think about my failures and regrets. Living here, I have learned that the old okes talk incessantly about their regrets. I stay away from the miserable ones. I prefer the ones who, instead of regretting, launch themselves into do-overs.

Take Ou Stephan from room 603. The old fool has convinced himself that Nurse Thandi will eventually fall for his charms. She will be his do-over from the choices he made in his youth. If you could call it a choice; the poor guy had no choice in the matter because it was simply unheard of, not to mention illegal, to run off with a kaffir in those days. Hell, he would have been disowned. Forty years later and he's hoping for the impossible, humbling like a fool while he's at it. He wears a full dress suit when Nurse Thandi is on duty and it is both sad and endearing to watch.

Nurse Thandi is in her prime and very much married, to a strapping guy who owns a gym. She plays along to make the old man happy and when her husband comes to pick her up, they spend time with Ou Stephan, who has begrudgingly accepted a friendship with Thandi's husband. They arm-wrestle in a test of strength and the young man lets him win. The old fool's delight at impressing Thandi reduces them to fits of giggles.

I am convinced that as we age we regress to our youth and our demons re-emerge stronger as our will to keep them in check weakens. I was a bully for as long as I could remember and the truth is I have no explanation for it. If you were to sit me down and ask me to explain why, I couldn't articulately pinpoint what it was. I just know that once I saw a person I had made a target to hurt, I felt exhilaration after inflicting the hurt. Like I had accomplished something and I would then calm down and be fine again. I also knew every time that it wouldn't be the last time.

As a young boy at school, it took me no time to realize that my easiest targets were girls because they scared easily. Their fear fed me but I soon got bored with the girls. Then I started bullying boys, the timid, quiet ones, and those who could stand up to me, I befriended. It was a game that spilled into my adult life until I had to face the hard knocks that tempered me into a man I never thought I would become.

A fatherly type figure, a trainer of young police officers and an adviser to senior structures of law enforcement. I'm convinced that behind my warm exterior, the young officers knew and could see the glint in my eyes of my capability to inflict pain, just not the extent of it.

Taming this volatile mean streak in me was a balancing act that took me down many winding roads, from a position of fists up and defensiveness, to open and active listening before responding. Finding stability was all thanks to Kristina's level-headed teachings and she raised me until our catastrophic fight and fall-out. There was a time from the age of eighteen into my mid-30s, when I couldn't even bring myself to remember her. I tried to forget her otherwise I would have been even more lost. But when I needed to remember her I did, and that is why I am looking forward to reuniting with her in the hereafter. To thank her for the seeds of survival she planted in my young pliable mind.

≡

I am feeling unusually nervous and anxious to meet my new nurse. I hope she is prepared to deal with my demons. It is exactly six o'clock when there is a knock at my door. In walks a figure of calmness that immediately drains away all the tension from my old muscles. The unmistaken scent of lavender wafts in with her. She seems to be all legs in those white pants of hers and I'm at a loss. My strategy was to dominate her from the minute she walked in but I feel like a shy boy on his first day of school.

"Well, what have we here, Mkhulu?" she says comically.

"I was expecting an old man but I see a young Hercules in front of me. My name is Zoe Zondi and I will be your night nurse for the next six months that I am here." She extends her hand and meets my eyes dead on, not in a challenging way but in a reading-the-mood sort of way. And right there it seems that I am completely disarmed by her. I know instantly that it's not a fluke. I can see the girl has a way with the people, a tool she knows she has in her bag. One that she uses ever so gently and naturally that it passes over those who are not observant. Hell, my job was to be observant. I played good cop, bad cop for years. I know people. I know how they shape-shift, how they manipulate and how they can be like a breath of cool, fresh air like this girlie. I was expecting a wet-behind-the-ears, skittish and smiley whimsical woman, but I am taken aback by the mystery of this one. She is strong in her presence and preserved in that ageless way that Black women so often are.

She confidently states what she is there for and it seems that I am not given any choice to decline or even be belligerent towards her. When I tell you that I am deurmekaar confused, I am. I take her slender warm hand and I almost curtsy. Mumbling something to her, I am outplayed before the game even begins.

"Much obliged, my Girlie."

I catch myself too late and wince at the term "my Girlie." These days I never know what could be taken as inappropriate. I have burned myself one too many times with machismo. If she notices, she doesn't show it or protest at what soon becomes my term of endearment for her.

≡

Slowly the cloudy mist that visits me in the night gently shifts and I can breathe easier and deeper. I always notice this when I first meet good people. When I meet troublemakers I get restless, the clouds close in on my chest and aggression grabs at my throat and that's when I turn into a monster. In my younger days I think this happened without me noticing. But since I clocked it, I use it as my compass. I navigate with it and I am almost always right. It is all in the eyes. When you stare at someone and prolong the hold, they shift uncomfortably. It's not that they are shy; it's that as you clock them, they clock you clocking them. Some people know it immediately while others suffer a feeling of unease they cannot place. I don't know who I empathize with the most, the ones who know or the ones who feel for the walls in the dark.

It is with this brief cloak-and-dagger approach that I saw it that first day I met Zoe. Her smile is broad and open but her eyes unmistakably know and see more than meets the eye. She is not the one who feels for the walls in the dark. She knows how to dance with the mood of a seemingly frightened old man. First be friendly, but ready to tackle those demons. I am sure she was briefed, diplomatically of course, but she knows the lingo. "Senile old white man with episodes" means we are putting you to the test to see if you can pacify an old sore bear.

I wish I could tell you that there was a long drawn-out battle of the wills between me and Zoe. I was almost disappointed that she passed the litmus test so easily. I admit that ageing softens even the die-hards like yours truly. We become putty in the hands of any feminine attention. They are not called life-givers for nothing.

Zoe's warmth left me feeling slightly shy and awkward but her easy, engaging manner drew me out of my discomfort. I felt seen in a way I don't think I have ever been before. At school, teachers saw me when I did well or misbehaved, at work I was seen for being a hard-nosed ass and, later on at the police academy, students saw me as an authority. Women I have been with me saw me just for the carnal spark between us, but with Zoe I am seen, really seen, as a human being. There was nothing she needed from me other than for me to be comfortable and warm and well. The light of this new way of being seen made me want to hide but I also knew I needed it. There's something to be said about that feeling and I wish it upon everyone, even if it is for a brief passing moment.

$$\equiv$$

We sit drinking hot chocolate, hers with no sugar and mine with two heaped teaspoons. As we age we go back to childhood delicacies and the nurses have spared me the lecture about the evilness of sugar. I like her even more for not batting an eye at my request to add sugar to my warm drink. We became acquainted in that easy but slightly guarded sort of way. The silences weren't awkward and we sipped our drinks and listened to the light January rain that was adding its magic to the familiar atmosphere between us.

Zoe reminded me of my students at the police academy and she brought on a strange longing for the grandchildren I have never met but dream of. Regrets of old cronies and forgotten friendships nestle in a bittersweet sensation that lulled me into a peaceful sleep that night. There was no episode the night I met Zoe, the girlie with big brown eyes and a warm smile. Did I mention her dry sense of humor that got me cackling while only her eyes did the smiling as she sipped on her hot chocolate? This became our nocturnal ritual; finding safety in hot chocolate regardless of the weather outside. When the heat outside was unbearable she would make a cold chocolate drink for herself while I still insisted on my hot chocolate. I am a creature of habit.

It's ironic that I could stick to something so loyally when I walked out on first Kristina and then my wife and son. I suppose it is easier to stick it out with things that give you pleasure but don't talk back. It is another story when they are human and can talk back and don't always give you the pleasure you desire in the way you want it, like a cup of hot chocolate.

I worked out by the end of the first week that Zoe reminded me so much of Kristina, the woman who raised me. She was just the right combination of firm and gentle. What are the odds of being ushered into this world by a wise soul and be ushered out of it by another? I am fully aware that this is the last stage of my life and I have chosen to revel in it in my moments of lucidity.

There were bets that Zoe wouldn't last more than a month but within a week it was clear that she had earned the respect and envy of her colleagues for being able to deal with a difficult old man like me. I no longer experienced my nocturnal nightmares and instead, if you stood in the garden below my window, you'd hear one of three things: my belly-aching laughter, my snores or simply silence. Silence was the loudest for those who knew me before Zoe came to chase away the darkness in me. The shadows were even leaving my face, according to the other old timers; the scowl was gone.

$$\equiv$$

I couldn't guess Zoe's age and at my age I know well enough to stay away from the topic of age with women. I am well versed in conversing indirectly to get information from people without invading the areas that are untouchable. Behind that smile, Zoe had waded through her own muddy waters and I think, like me, she took the lessons and locked the rest somewhere in the memory of "to be opened on rare occasions." My Florence Nightingale was a wounded healer and I liked that; the scars of war are an honorable thing.

What I did find out about Zoe is that she is a consummate traveler and a seeker of life in surprising ways. She works six months of the year and travels the other six months, recording her adventures for news outlets that pay her good money. She is offered sponsorships from all sorts of companies for mention in her videos and her resourcefulness earned my respect. I felt proud of her and I wasn't even her real mkhulu. I can see why she gets paid top dollar; the girl had a way with words while still earnestly connecting in a girl-next-door sort of way.

I don't know if my storytelling comes from Kristina and my Oumagrootjie or if it developed with my prompting when taking statements in police stations, but I love a good story that gets you right from the beginning. I spent my days on the computer reading about Zoe's adventures and I found all her essays engaging. I can almost hear her steady, unhurried voice in them. During the day I read about her and at night I sat with her and heard her voice spin her story.

ZOE

MY BIRTH WAS contentious and fraught with complications but I was the answer my mother wanted from God. She wanted a baby to cement her relationship with her mother-in-law, my Gogo Tu, and it worked like a charm. The insults stopped and I was the apple of my Gogo's eye and my mother finally solidified her status as a proper childbearing makoti, not a modern girl who took her only son away from his mother. It was the classic story of a mother who didn't see her son's wife as an addition to the family but as competition for his affections. It is a thing in so many families where mothers don't know how to let go of their sons.

Gogo Tu later told me how she struggled to believe that my mother had no intentions of hurting my father and so she was fiercely protective of him. My father was born with a lightning mark on his face so his right eye was grey and he had a patch of white on the right side of his forehead up to his hairline and a patch of jarring white hair. It was an unusual contrast to his perfectly dark skin and, as a result, he grew up the butt of jokes at school. But his sense of humor and talent at playing soccer created a space for him to belong. It's just as well he had a sense of humor because if he didn't he would have looked decidedly frightening. His easy smile made him likeable and popular as a young man.

Back then in his community only a few families were not Catholic and so when her son chose a girl who was not only not Catholic but also fatherless and the daughter of a woman who came into town scandalized, Gogo Tu felt sure that doom had knocked on her door.

My maternal grandmother had tried to outrun her problems after discovering that she was pregnant with my mother. She had lived with a monster who ran his household like an army; he was a teacher by day, a preacher on Sundays and a sick, twisted monster at night. He found himself between his teenage stepdaughter's thighs, violating her and crying apologies afterwards, promising it wouldn't happen again, saying the devil made him do it. It was pointless for my grandmother to tell her mother because she was under his spell and hopeless to fight him off. Her mother worshipped him and didn't even address him as "husband" but as "father."

When my grandmother found out she was pregnant something turned. She knew she had an auntie who hated this man. It was never talked about but she knew that her auntie had had run-ins with him, which led to a split between twin sisters. It was a family secret and some believed my great-aunt was jealous of her sister for finding an educated man of God, despite having a child out of wedlock. My grandmother worked out that her auntie knew there was something sinister with this teacher-man-of-God-monster and had tried warning her sister but it caused problems so she let her sister be.

My grandmother planned her great escape and found refuge with her renegade auntie who lived among my paternal Gogo's community. She was known for being vulgar and hers was one of the few families that were openly un-Catholic. When my grandmother finally gave birth to my mother, her auntie raised them both since my grandmother was also practically a child when she birthed my mother at fifteen. It was a house of women.

She forced my grandmother to go back to school and finish her education, which she did and thrived, but depression was a constant thorn in her side. The tradition of nursing began in my family when my grandmother trained as a nurse and my mother followed in her footsteps, which is how she met my father. She was eighteen and he was twenty-two. He came howling into the emergency room with a broken ankle. He was a soccer player and had fallen, with his opponent landing on top of him, leading to the sickening sound of his ankle breaking. He was rushed to Edendale Hospital from Wadley Stadium where the match was taking place.

My mother was a trainee nurse and on duty that night and she nursed him back to health. His favorite part of recovery in the hospital was draping his arm around my mother and having her help him walk the passages to gain his strength back. It was during these walks that they fell for each other. Six months into their romance and my father was ready to pay lobola and marry my mother. His mother was not the only one aggrieved by his decision; his soccer team felt he had dumped them for a girl. They had lost their "Jack London" as he was a big asset to the team. He used his broken ankle as an excuse not to play or practice but he was enjoying spending time with my mother and was completely taken by her.

Another hurdle my parents had to face was the priest, the red-faced Irish Father McCain who did not believe that my mother was eighteen years old. She looked much younger and he instructed her to convert to Catholicism and then wait a year before he would evaluate whether they were old and mature enough to get married. This angered my father who served every Sunday as an altar boy in the church. My mother agreed to convert despite her great-aunt's protestations. My father knew that Father McCain could be instructed by the diocese bishop so he calmly thanked the priest for his advice and mentioned that he would have a talk with the bishop in Durban. He would request that the bishop officiate the wedding because as far as he was concerned they had followed all the instructions they had been given. The color drained from the priest's face and his arrogance tempered slightly.

"No need to take such drastic measures, son. What's the rush? Aye, I will look into my schedule and come back to you with a date. December you said, right? Alright then sonny, calm down. I will make myself available."

And so it was that in December 1969 my mother and

father walked down the aisle, beaming with joy and triumph to stand in front of brandy-soaked Father McCain to say, "I do." Gogo Tu shrugged off her misgivings on her son's big day and joyously ululated along with the rest of the community.

When two whole years passed without any sign of pregnancy, Gogo Tu began her smear campaign and dropped hints that my mother was using contraceptives, a scandalous thing for a good Catholic. She said my mother was too modern for her taste. What was my mother waiting for? Marriage was for childbearing, not frolicking and romancing her son like white people do. She reminded my mother that the Catholic Church is against prevention and my mother would pray and cry for a child. They were a rough two years marked by the sudden death of my maternal grandmother. She was found sleeping peacefully having taken an overdose of pills with a note asking for forgiveness. She had endured the trauma of her youth with grit and determination to see her daughter succeed, to see her happy walking down the aisle and was convinced that she had served her debt to humanity. My mother's great-auntie also lost her will to live shortly thereafter.

$$\equiv$$

My father had his first adult quarrel with his mother and told her to butt out of his marriage and stop the demands for grandchildren; they would come when they were ready. He was fiercely protective of my mother, especially since she had lost all her family. Things were strained until one day

my mother came home from work on top of the moon as she
had found out that she was pregnant. The icy relationship
thawed between the two women and Gogo Tu became
tender towards my mother. I was named Life, or Zoe,
because I had brought life into family. At seven days old I
was dressed in a long white christening gown and presented
to Father McCain with all the other infants to be baptized.
My mother sat with the other moms, all cradling their
bundles of joy and next to her was her best friend with her
baby boy, Blessing. Apparently we stretched out our stubby
little hands and clasped at each other and it became a joke
growing up that we took to each other at seven days old.

Another childhood story we share and that Gogo Tu
loved repeating happened on my fifth birthday when all
the children were gathered to celebrate my day with me.
Blessing, or Bhoyi as we called him, wanted to sit next to
me but my best friend Sindi had already claimed the seat
and wouldn't budge. I was a hot ticket that day and because
it was my birthday the cake and sweets and presents were
all mine and everyone wanted to be my friend or was
possessive of me. When Bhoyi asked Sindi to shift from the
seat next to me she said, "No, she is my best friend, you can
sit over there."

Bhoyi shot back, "Well she may be your best friend
but she will be my wife when we get older," and stuck his
tongue out at her. That story never failed to mortify Bhoyi
when we were older.

On hearing that Bhoyi wanted to marry me, I went
straight to his mother and said, "Auntie, can Bhoyi stay with
us as my husband from today?" When the adults laughed

and didn't give me a straight answer, sugar-high Bhoyi and I decided we would hot foot it and run away from home together. We marched to the adults hand in hand and announced that we were leaving because they wouldn't let us get married. Bhoyi and I were like the same person but with two hearts.

The first time I saw him peeing standing up, I stared and stared but I didn't say anything. He seemed upset, like me seeing him pee offended him. Later that afternoon when Gogo Tu was giving us cookies and Oros, Bhoyi asked Gogo, who might as well have been his gogo because we spent so much time with her, "Gogo Tu, how come Zoe's hoo-ha is so strange? She pees sitting down." Gogo laughed so hard we ended up laughing too, not knowing what was so funny. The only clue was that it had to do with Bhoyi's question.

$$\equiv$$

Gogo looked after me, Bhoyi and Sindi like we were all her grandchildren and we were so close it was like we were triplets. But when we became teenagers, things got complicated. Sindi and I quickly became guarded with each other and no longer shared everything with one another. The competition she had with Bhoyi for my affections when we were children became a competition between her and I for Bhoyi's affection. He was smart and funny and I was suspicious that Sindi liked him like I did. Sindi was beautiful and I felt insecure, like I had come up short compared to her. I refused to question who Bhoyi liked though and that threatened to undo me and my lifelong friendships.

Things were happening so quickly in our lives at this stage. Bhoyi was the natural leader of our group at school and he was like a shape-shifter who could switch from being the class clown to being so stubborn he could shut down a history lesson if he didn't agree with the teacher. Bhoyi knew things about history that we didn't know and he didn't mince words with our teacher, who always tried to stick to what was legally prescribed in the syllabus.

That is how we all became politically aware and realized that there were things that we were not being told. I didn't know anything then but I knew Bhoyi was onto something and I loved him even more for it. There was something more than that though and it was the biology of my hormones. I was smitten. Bhoyi's confidence is what made him attractive to me. Girls my age only went for looks so if it had been about that I would have gone for his friend, Freedom, who had girls scratching each other for his attention, but it was more than that. Later on I found out that my suspicions were correct and that Sindi was also nursing a secret crush on Bhoyi.

Bhoyi was tall and so dark even his gums were Black and they were always on display because he laughed so much. As soon as Sindi started noticing boys, Bhoyi became her fixation. What she had for him was more than a crush; she obsessed over him. If she saw Bhoyi laughing with another girl, and that happened often, her day was ruined. She would run into the school's smelly bucket toilet, close the door and try to calm down by breathing in and out. This was a difficult thing to do since taking gulps of air in there was like inhaling methane gas.

Sindi was a beautiful girl who had to dodge the attention of teachers, older men and even the paws of patrolling police who were all over our township dealing with the state of emergency at the time. We lived like hunted animals with the political situation as it was. Sindi was light in skin color, which meant she could pass as colored, drawing men to her like bees to honey. The lingering eyes of old men, young men, fat men, thin men, none of whom would ever admit to it. This made Sindi weary and withdrawn. When she spoke, everyone seemed to listen because they automatically thought she was clever because she was light-skinned and therefore "more white." It was a mystery that always intrigued Sindi about Black people, that in their waking hours they were harassed, forced to call white people "Madam" and "Sir," tortured, raped, have their land stolen, their livelihoods denied, yet they continued to view whiteness with reverence. As the epitome of what it means to be beautiful and the means to a more sophisticated life.

Sindi and I were both wary of men. While their eyes fixated on Sindi's delicate, pale skin, their eyes hardened on me. There was something of a visceral nature about me that threatened them. I was a different type of feminine and while they wanted to make love to Sindi, they wanted to fuck me like a dog. While township men wanted to marry someone like me, many wanted to experience having sex with someone like Sindi and brag about it later. We didn't have to be told any of this; we felt it in their gaze. We were always in danger so we hid ourselves behind our clothes and evaded any male glances. Sindi clung to the warmth of our friendship. I was a little older than her and we were in contrast to one another in many ways, not just because I was darker and taller than her. We knew nothing of a Black Madonna when we were growing up but we often heard men passing salacious comments.

$$\equiv$$

Bhoyi, Freedom, Sindi and I formed a group, not only because we were childhood friends but one shaped by the politics of the day and the sexual tension of youth. We wanted to skip the country and train for war against the police state that was our South Africa at the time. Bhoyi and Freedom were already part of the UDF community patrols and other secret activities involving the stockpiling of guns Police and young soldiers terrorized us on our streets. Boys ran from police and dropped pistols or banned books in the water tins that girls carried on their heads walking from the communal tap to their homes.

"I don't know about you lot but me, I will not cower to the police dogs," Bhoyi ranted. "I will die standing so you decide about the future of this country, I am skipping as soon as I get a chance. The garbage they are feeding us at school is not the full truth. I mean look at our church. Why do we have a statue of a white man hanging there as our Jesus? The God in my dream is as Black as me."

Bhoyi got heated and he wanted us to go with him. He felt anchored when we were all together. Freedom was the quiet and thoughtful one in the group, steady and as loyal as a dog. I could count on him to keep the group grounded. I knew Bhoyi so well and I knew he was afraid that the authorities were coming for us. I decided to join Bhoyi because school wouldn't be the same without him and I couldn't bear the thought of not seeing him every day. I told Sindi that I was going to go with Bhoyi and she wrestled with her decision whether to come too for a full three months, but I didn't lose patience. I knew her well and she always took her time with everything and was calm and steady.

Then one day it happened swiftly, just as Bhoyi had said it would, and it tore us apart. The police grabbed Bhoyi by the scruff of his neck and threatened to shoot him for not addressing them as "Sir." The community watched and grumbled quietly but knew better than to try intervene. As the sounds of slap after slap rained down on Bhoyi, no one moved an inch.

"Just say it, Bhoyi, say 'Sir' and save yourself!" shouted one woman.

But Bhoyi stayed mum. His sense of humor was gone but his dignity was intact. His silence terrified the angry policeman and he became rougher. The other two policemen grew uneasy at the sight of Black men standing and watching one of their own being humiliated. The policeman eventually grew tired and bored of Bhoyi's defiance and casually pulled out his gun and cut down Bhoyi's life right there.

Freedom was at the top of the bridge when he saw what happened and took out his own gun. He fired and the bullet rocketed and hit the policeman between his eyes. The policeman's eyes widened as he realized what was happening, a curse forming on his lips as he fell down next to Bhoyi's beautiful muscle-toned body lying crumpled on the floor. There was a thudding sound as the fallen policeman hit the ground, thick red blood pouring out of his head. In the end it didn't matter, Bhoyi's blood mingled with the policeman's in the middle of the madness.

Bhoyi was defiant, even in death, as he jerked and gasped for air. By now, the other two policemen were surrounded. They backed into their vehicle while a crowd of Black men, emboldened by the actions of a calculating teenager, advanced slowly towards them, their anger rising and jaws clenched. Women were screaming and wailing for Bhoyi. Freedom came down from the bridge and ran to Bhoyi's body. He scooped him into his arms and pleaded for his comrade to hang on, even though he knew that Bhoyi was gone. Seeing red, he turned to the gasping and dying policeman and shot him again and again. The crowd had surrounded the yellow van and the two white figures inside the van were pale with terror. The driver revved the engine as the crowd banged the van and rocked it back and forth. The policeman in the passenger seat was crying and eventually the van shot forward and accelerated out of the Caluza location.

Sindi's house was near the road and she witnessed it all. Acid bile built up in her chest and burned her throat. She stood shaking. The tragedy of it all was the stupidity of the egos of everyone involved. The man who was driven to kill because a kaffir did not call him "Sir" and a young man preferring death rather than humoring one more insecure asshole in his life.

Bhoyi had witnessed more police brutality than he

cared to remember and this was just one time too many. He learned early on how to soften the hard blows of humiliation just like his father used to do when he cracked a joke and led the laughter to show the kids that everything was okay. Bhoyi and his siblings laughed because laughter was contagious but they knew something was very wrong. Bhoyi always looked at his mother, who laughed until tears came streaming down. He knew they were not tears of happiness but he couldn't work out if they were tears of anger, relief or fear. He knew that his day of humiliation was coming and he wouldn't laugh that day.

$$=$$

Sindi was shaking with emotion on the day of Bhoyi's funeral. Shaking with fear, hate, anger and the hopelessness of it all. We comforted each other and she steadied my trembling hand and held it between hers. She sang until all the mourners went quiet and turned to look at where the angelic voice they were hearing was coming from. She closed her eyes and transported herself to the future and the freedom she was singing about. "Somedaaaay we shall overcome, deep in my heart I do believe that we shall overcome some day. The Lord shall set us free, the Lord shall set us free."

Suddenly her singing was interrupted by the deafening sound of gunshots. Freedom had pulled out his gun and fired shots in the air.

"Bullshit, Sindi," he screamed. "It is this bazooka that will set us free. The Lord is on *their* side. They made the agreement with the Lord and they believe they are the chosen ones. Look around you. On Sundays they go to their Lord and thank him for the food they have, at our expense, and for the maids who clean up after them. The Lord, my beautiful sister, is not on your side. He, she or it never was!" Hot tears choked him and he looked demented with pain. He dropped the gun on the ground, screaming and howling until he fell into the arms of his big-bosomed auntie who rocked him to her like a child.

Tears flowed throughout the congregation. Tears for Bhoyi and tears for Freedom. Tears of pain. Bhoyi was loved and in his short eighteen years of life his wit and humor touched, charmed and brought a smile to many.

After the funeral, Sindi and I talked about our fears. Something about death expands and opens the heart and we exchanged all our secrets. We discovered that we had both lost our virginity to Bhoyi and knew our love was our strength. We knew it was time to join the others. We knew we needed to cross the border and fight.

"Praying for relief is not the answer, Zoe, we have to fight," said Sindi. She said it with fervor in her eyes and I agreed. Late into the night, once the intensity of emotion was wearing down, Sindi asked, "Zoe, what about Gogo Tu? Who will look after her?"

The pain of hearing that question being verbalized took my breath away. I was quiet for a while before answering the question with another question.

"I know Freedom thinks God is against us but he's wrong. God's eye is on all of us and he cares about us and hears our cries. Unlike them who pray to God alone, we have ancestors and my mother's spirit has never left us. She will look after her own. Have you ever seen a sparrow going unfed?"

My mother had helped many men escape the police from the hospital she worked at. There was a network of cleaners, nurses and doctors who helped men who had been caught and injured to recover and skip the country. When the police realized what was happening, there was a mass incarceration of all those involved in the operation. My mother was caught, beaten and raped and later found dead in a cell, the police sheepishly claiming she had committed suicide. My father was beside himself with grief and never recovered.

"Suicide! They say my wife committed suicide but did she have to shed all her clothes and spread her legs if she was going to kill herself? Her arms and legs were tied to the post of the bed. How do you kill yourself when you are tied up like that?" He told everyone how he was called to claim his wife's body and how the police could not look him in the eye. That they were like dogs that had eaten their own. He had a breakdown and was eventually committed to a psychiatric institution.

$$\equiv$$

It was time. We had talked about it enough and knew we would not be like our placid elders who simply shrugged and said one day things would be better. Sindi was more cerebral in her thinking and reasoning while Freedom was ready to skip the border the very next day. Sindi wanted to process it all and see that her conviction went beyond her grief of losing Bhoyi. I waited patiently because I knew Sindi was ready and she knew that the solution was to take up arms and leave the country, but I also knew that what was stalling her decision was the worry and concern about those we left behind. We couldn't tell anyone even if we wanted to. It was for our safety and the safety of the network that was assisting all those who were fleeing the country. It was an elaborate network from northern Natal into Swaziland and into Mozambique, where we would be grilled with questions until it was clear that we were not double agents.

$$=$$

The night we decided to leave, I cooked supper for Gogo Tu and I waited for the signal from Freedom, but it never came. I couldn't sleep and lay awake all night not knowing what had happened. The next day at school, Sindi and Freedom were nowhere to be found. My classroom had ten empty seats that day, even Zumpu the math whiz had gone.

"Ah, even our math whiz is gone," our teacher shook his head sadly and said nothing more.

I was too numb to cry. My heart felt bruised and I felt like I had to do everything slowly to prevent it from shriveling up. I was sadness itself. I looked and smelled of sadness and I think all of us who were left felt the same. Everyone I knew had been touched by the hand of death, the multiple deaths of friends and relatives.

Years later I found out that Sindi and Freedom had

made one of the hardest decisions of their lives that night. They had to leave me behind because when they came for me, they saw the police patrolling my street. They had no choice but to leave me behind. My final year at school was a blur and I felt so alone and dead inside.

MADALA

I WAS SO shocked by what Zoe had told me that I couldn't even look at her. My throat seized up and tears that had been locked inside me started flowing and they kept coming. I was a mess and before Zoe left, she petted my hand and wiped her own tears.

"Don't you start with me, old man, because if I break down now I don't know if I will be able to stop!" We both do that ugly laugh-cry thing that I never used to understand and it feels both good and heavy. Zoe kneels next to my bed and we cry together. It's a release that I didn't even know I needed and something I had never done in my eighty years. I finally meet her big brown eyes, bloodshot from crying, and she meets my eyes and nods. Like she can hear me even though I haven't spoken. She nods again and says, "We wear many masks, Mkhulu. Thank you for letting me put mine down for a bit and for showing me your face without your mask. I am sure you were a beautiful little boy; I saw a glimpse of him today. We are made of madness, Mkhulu. Madness. Underneath the veneer of our manicured lawn is a soup of maggots and dormant lava of hot red pain."

She tucks me in and leaves me curled up in the fetal position under the bedcovers. I don't want to look at her again, not trusting that my voice will not break and I will crumble to pieces if I utter a single word. Thin, cold rain weeps with me and I feel a little afraid, like something is standing outside my window. I want a warm body beside me so I take a pillow and squeeze it to me until I am lulled into a serene sleep. I wake up the next morning feeling renewed but also ravenous. There's something about letting go of emotion that feels like you've smoked a fat joint of really good stuff from Swaziland.

I feel emptied of baggage but listening to the news that morning quickly fills me with trepidation. At some point I have to open up my own can of worms. A flu-like virus is killing people overseas and there are talks of shutting things down to avoid the spreading of infection. Many of the old timers here have children living overseas and there are tearful assurances back and forth. Some do not believe it and are convinced their children are abandoning them. I go back and hide in my space after my breakfast. Too much is happening too fast and I'm glad my Girlie has a long weekend off. I want time to read and be alone. She has left me able to cope with my night fears. Whenever she leaves, just as I am falling asleep hovering between the living and the dead, she whispers in my ear, "You are safe, Mkhulu." I never fail to hear it and soon enough the fluttering bird in my chest quietens. I finally believe her and, even in the thick of a nightmare, I remember that I am safe. It has become a way to wake myself up from a nightmare or break the paralysis of a lucid dream.

I begin to wonder about Zoe's friends and whether they made it out or if they are just bones scattered somewhere. I stop myself because I can't let my mind wander, knowing what we used to do to those young and frightened children. We used to feed on their fear and thrive on breaking those filled with youthful bravado.

I know that you cannot kill another without killing bits of yourself in the process. There are many of us, walking zombies, who may have evaded the law and the TRC but are in the loop of our own torturous Groundhog Day. Killing children felt like hundreds of tiny spiders crawling and boring themselves into my soul. When Mandela took over and we saw a new class of Blacks moving into our suburbs, we saw children speaking like ours, befriending our children, and we were emboldened. We thought it was fair and square and that we could move on. We hung onto that rainbow carpet to hide our infestation. Some of us old guard sat and ate with the new guard at the table of the new day. I have watched the scramble for a seat at the table that still leaves many feeling like the seat has been pulled out from under them. I had no way of knowing how it could be righted so I turned a blind eye and hogged my share.

In the first ten years of the new dispensation, I fell into a role of managing the nervous skittishness of others like me who were still in the force. I was at the headquarters, having transferred from Natal, and there was an air of distrust among us. But we gravitated to our smoke room together and tried to boost each other's morale. We became a cabal that gathered to smoke and engage in self-pity. We were afraid and unclear about our future with a Black president and Black seniors who were mostly returnees from exile. It was a smokescreen and a game I knew well.

The room would be thick with smoke as we dragged on one Stuyvesant cigarette after another. Outside of those four walls, some were jokers who learned to blend in with the new Black executives. Others, who didn't have the skill or the stomach for brown-nosing, kept under the radar, doing what needed to be done to get to pension day. They were polite and took orders with "Sir" or "Mam" at the end of every sentence. We held out and could see the light at the end of the tunnel but it was the last few steps that were the most difficult. Our pensions were inching close to the millions and we were determined to get to that last day in one piece.

I would tell them all that everyone has a price, you just need to find the gap and exploit the hell out of it. Even the most hard-ass person melts when they see a white man give them respect. Nothing matters more to them than to feel that they are being heard, recognized and respected by their former oppressors. Say "Sir" or "Mam" and see them puff up with pride and their resolve soften.

Old Kobus used to give the okes a pep talk that helped me find my way. He was a solid man, a man with a plan, and I'm glad I listened to him because it paid off.

"Check your pride at the door, mense, and let's think about our retirement," he would say. "Meneer Mandela has given us a chance, let's not ruin it by showing our hand too soon. The time will come when we can say, 'Fuck you very much I'm out of here.' The day I turn sixty, I'll get my payout, take what's mine and sail away with Mariette somewhere far away from here. Listen to me carefully, especially those of you who still have a decade to put up with this place before you cash in. They talk tough about their Africanism but pay attention to their actions, neh. Look, their children can't speak their own languages anymore and it's been a little under a decade since they took over. Half of their men dropped their Black wives as soon as the laws changed and they moved to the suburbs. Black educated ladies are keen on white boys too, hey. Watch how the women treat each other with contempt and how everything is a competition. They size each other up with coldness and are like fierce cats; only the strong survive. Most of these guys choose to have a white PA!"

We all laughed in unison, recalling an eminent minister who told anyone who would listen that he had a "White woman secretary who makes tea for me. A white madam makes tea for me! Come and visit me and you can see for yourself. I'm telling you, comrade, things have changed, we have our country back." It was like a validation of his power and status. That minister was a clown and gave us plenty to chuckle about. There was almost a practiced look of indifference towards whoever seemed to be intellectually superior to them. Like there was a memo that said never, under any circumstances, show that you are impressed by anyone because it will show that you are weak. Hell, they even had a word for it, the "PHD syndrome" or the "pull him/her down syndrome."

Kobus carried on. "Now they're all sipping Moët and Irish whiskey, wearing Swiss watches, eating sushi, driving big German cars, living in Sandton, Houghton and Morningside and their kids go to Crawford College, Michaelhouse and St Anne's. They wear only the best Brazilian wigs and use Caro Light to lighten their skins. Heck, some even go under the knife to have their broad noses sliced thin and all of a sudden they've developed posh accents! They want to be like us. Don't let their 'rah-rah Black is beautiful' crap shake you. Give them what they want, feed their egos with affirmation, praise them for the ideas that were actually yours and make it seem like they came up with them. Look, truth be told, some of these young Black graduates coming up are sharper than us, but management will never take their ideas seriously because they are Black like them."

I knew what he was talking about because there had many times when someone gave me their report and told me to put my name on it. "Hey Madala, we know they'll lap it up coming from you." Those used to be the most uncomfortable presentations, taking credit away from them because their own seniors wouldn't recognize the brilliance of their work. They'd fall for my old ideas hook, line and sinker and I even managed to resuscitate a few from back in the day and change a word here and there. They'd buy it because it came from me. Because I am an institutional memory.

"Never underestimate the social capital that your pale skin still holds in this country, mense," said Kobus, interrupting my thoughts. "Even those who claim to hate us, on a subconscious level we still have them by their big Black balls. The key is to be charming because if you're arrogant, you'll make them angry and you don't want that. It's like when you confront a snake. You don't run at it, you stand still and that's when you strike it on the head. This game of survival is mental, okes. Trust me, I'm old and I have seen a thing or two. You need to be their right-hand person. They need to rely on you so much that they wouldn't know how to shit without you around. Why do you think I'm still the chief's right-hand man? Even with the moratorium that bars us from getting higher positions."

"Ja, Kobus man," interjected Jakob Greyling, another one of the old guard waiting to pension out. "You see that's the difference between a Boer and an Afrikaner. I'm a Boer and you're an Afrikaner, with all your liberal tendencies. I hear you, you kiss ass and it has worked for you, but jirre dit is mos very, very difficult for me to watch silly kaffirs playing big and expect me to play along. It is damn well near fokken impossible, okes."

Poor Jakob was cracking under all the pressure. He was working with a tough one who was not readable like the others. She did her homework and wasn't easily fooled. No wig on her head, not a smudge of make-up on her face, she had no interest in men, Black or white, and so he had no chance of ingratiating himself into her good books. She wasn't mean, just plain indifferent.

We couldn't take indifference; an indifferent Black senior was deadly. We wanted to be able to handle them and be in control. It was all a subtle psychological dance. It had been drilled into our heads that we needed to always be in control and in a position of superiority, even in situations where we had to play along. We could play along as long as we had the feeling of having the upper hand.

There were five of us oldies left at the headquarters and we were just hanging on. Jakob was hanging on by the skin of his teeth and was always hovering close to losing it. He couldn't take the umlungu jokes and he couldn't handle the attitudes of the new shiny Black youth who were joining the force and messing up the traditions he loved and had served under since he left the army. Being in law enforcement had run in his family for as long as he could remember.

Jakob made us all nervous and a few times we had to step in when we saw the word "kaffir" forming on his lips during some heated moments. His unsmiling woman boss demanded work and it "de-whitened" and emasculated him at the same time. He was always on edge and sitting in traffic jams between Joburg and Pretoria, he constantly ended up in road-rage clashes.

$$\equiv$$

A few days after our talk with Kobus, Jakob headed back to his office after his lunch break and found all his belongings packed into boxes. He was being moved to the basement where there was not a single white policeman. "Fokken kaffir bitch." There it was, like glass shattering on the floor. He screamed it down the passage and everyone came out of their offices. He had a moerse epic meltdown, kicked his desk, threw his papers and marched towards the boss's office. But everyone rushed to guard her door and the young ones laughed openly, "Ayeye ngamla, ayeye, for once we are getting your honest feelings, Ayoba."

We all heard the commotion and ran into the corridor. "Oh fok," Kobus muttered and quickly grabbed Jakob and pinned him against the wall. He was grunting and fighting to free himself. "Los dit man, Kobus! I'm out of this shit hole. Fucking stinking Blacks who think they can run this country! You are nothing without us you bloody bastards! You'll never succeed you corrupt chumps! The only decent thing you can claim for yourself is Mandela, that's it!" He was raging with anger. Attempts to cover his mouth didn't stop him and eventually he marched to his car and drove away. Kobus and I tailed him to make sure he didn't do anything stupid. We were still shocked by his outburst and lost in our own thoughts, wondering what he would do next. He ended up at Lynnwood Bridge Mall and bought a bottle of Klipdrift to drink himself silly. He also had the added stress that his sister Hannetjie, who was married to the Black Minister of Education, had recently been diagnosed with cancer.

As if his day couldn't get any worse, Jakob then spotted his brother-in-law, Freedom, in the shopping center, sitting with a woman and a child at Rhapsody restaurant. He started to hyperventilate when he heard the child call Freedom "Papa" and Freedom only clocked Jakob when he was nearly at their table.

"Ja, né, swaer. My sister is battling for her life and here you are having a cozy lunch with your kaffirbitch and kaffirtjie here!" Jakob is having epic meltdown number two and this time it turns physical. He takes aim, attempting to knock Freedom's lights out for fooling around on his sister. But he misses and the full might of a two-meter tall, more than 150-kilogram policeman's punch, lands on the child instead. She flies up in the air, hitting the glass door behind her and smashes her head and then falls to the concrete floor. She's unconscious before she hits the ground.

Mayhem ensues as security guards run to try restrain the mad policeman. There is a hushed silence in the restaurant as Jakob is taken away kicking and screaming, accusing Freedom of being a "fokken kaffir cheating on his sister and giving her AIDS."

Like blow flies sensing shit and decay, members of the media materialize and start taking pictures and asking questions about the big government official's love scandal. What would sell more papers than the headline "High-ranking official caught with his pants down" even though Freedom was completely clothed in his navy blue Prada suit, sitting in a restaurant eating lunch? "Philandering minister gives his white wife AIDS" some papers led with the next day, no verification needed.

The minister is shell-shocked and completely immobile. He can't even get into the ambulance with his daughter because members of the press are blocking his way.

≡

Kobus and I see all of this happen but we are helpless to do anything and get out of there as fast as we can. We can't get mixed up with anything that would get us into the papers. Jakob would have to face the consequences alone.

"The show is over mense, nothing to see here," says the restaurant manager. "I'm going to have to ask you to leave my property. Minister, please come this way to my office.

Petros, take care of the cleaning up and count the damages for me, okay?"

The restaurant manager, who had secretly tipped off the media, played the role of the savior. He "rescued" the minister and got security to chase away the hacks. He was a savvy businessman. Free publicity for his restaurant and his "act of kindness" meant a lot of business for him in the future with plenty of big cheeses patronizing his bar and restaurant with their big shiny gold cards and big tips. It was a win all around.

$$\equiv$$

My hot chocolate was turning cold sitting on my night table undrunk. There were so many memories and my heart was heavy with remembering. I know the shock Zoe would feel if she knew all my stories. I feel hopeless and the relief and release I had with her is gone. I'm ready to say goodbye.

But it's not my time. It's two months into Zoe's contract and talks of closing the country are heating up. I watched the coverage of those fires in Australia and it gave me a sinking feeling in my stomach. I thought about going there when I first retired and people I know have settled there. When the television beamed pictures of the flames engulfing the sky and the moon turning black, it looked beautiful and terrifying at same time; the undeniable flag of the Aboriginal people. Something more than just wildfires was going on there and I'm glad I stayed put.

I'm getting tired of the news always leaving me with a sense of dread. I couldn't really be bothered to listen about this damn flu but I know Zoe is concerned for her next trip overseas. I admit that a part of me wishes that her stay could be extended. She has become a beacon of hope for me and I'm already dreading the day she leaves, if I'm still alive.

I can't work out if Zoe's ease with people of any color is from her traveling or her nursing. I have watched her with others and she has no affectations, whether she's communicating with the cleaning staff, her other colleagues or Ms. Rajah. She is warm towards all of them and no one is on a pedestal. A rare gem, this girl, and I feel lucky that our relationship goes further than just small talk.

"Tell me this, my Girlie, did you take up nursing because it ran in the family or was it fate?" I can't help it. I'm like a moth to a flame and I need to hear more of this girl's story. Plus, I'm delaying her questions about my past.

ZOE

MKHULU WANTS TO know more and I feel comfortable enough to probe further into my past and my life story. He has triggered a recalling that is lightening my load.

"No Mkhulu, it was very intentional. I wanted to do it to honor my mother and grandmother but also because I watched the boy I loved die like a dog in front of me and my community. I remember thinking that if only I could have stopped the bleeding, if only I could have put him together again and made him laugh. But his face was still and I couldn't help him. That's why I wanted to be a nurse."

≡

It was a helluva journey to get where I am and reflecting back feels good. I studied nursing in the early nineties once I left school and I've worked as a nurse ever since. Those were bloody times in the hospitals. There was so much violence from the politics of power and fear-mongering. We stitched up gaping wounds, closed the eyes of dying youth and kept the secrets of people's last gasping confessions. It was fast and maddening, with no time to process it all. Our careers were limited to teaching, policing or nursing back then and you were lucky if you got to study medicine or law. I like people so I like being a nurse, especially now that I've worked out how to be a free agent and I get to engage both my passions and do what I love. Let's just say I became a nurse by design.

When Gogo Tu passed away, I left to go and work in England. They were giving two-year work visas to citizens of Commonwealth countries and so that was it for me. The traveling bug bit me hard. I caught buses and trains to criss-cross Europe on my vacations away from the hospital. In the back of my mind, wherever I went, I was always looking for Sindi and Freedom. Only Zumpu made it back from the group that skipped the border. He was damaged beyond repair and became the local drunk. He made it known that he fought for the Khongolose and would say, "When I die, you'll see, they'll bury me like a soldier." He would pump his chest and break into war songs and, true to his word, they did bury him with the pomp and ceremony given to a veteran. I couldn't entertain any thoughts of my friends lying dead in a ditch somewhere. It would have been too much. So I harbored hope and played a game in my head that we would all be reunited someday.

=

I realized I had a lot to learn when it came to traveling and I wasn't always the sophisticated traveler I am now. On my first plane trip, I blundered something chronic and exposed my country bumpkin self in ways that make me cringe when I think about it.

Firstly, my suitcase was a musty old voluminous second-hand thing that was falling apart. In my carry-on luggage, I packed some padkos of dombolo and tripe with a liter of gemmer, imagine! I can't believe I thought I would make it through security! I was livid and didn't believe the explanation they gave me. I'd been on plenty of trains and buses in my life, with padkos, and nobody had ever taken my food from me. I cringe now thinking about how I called the security official a food Nazi!

$$\equiv$$

Mkhulu and I laugh, belly-hurting and life-affirming cackles. It feels good to laugh with him and to be able to laugh at myself and my naïveté. In some ways, Mkhulu feels like a grandfather and it feels good to be telling my story. Plus, I know he's become attached to being called Mkhulu.

I think back to staying in the UK for about ten years and occasionally coming home to check on my father. But then I started to do the great migration thing and, like the birds, I heard the call to come home.

At first my father didn't know who I was because the medication had confused him after so many years. Occasionally he thought I was my mom until he remembered that she had died, and then the memories of how she died came flooding back and he'd get so upset they'd have to restrain him in a straitjacket. He was still living in the police state in his head and he was so frightened.

I decided to leave my job in the UK and I moved back home and into Gogo Tu's house, which had been looked after by a parishioner from her church. I wanted to be close to my father. We were heading into 2010 and the excitement of the Soccer World Cup. I was determined I was going to coax my father back to reality. But first I had to convince the hospital to give him a pass to allow him to come and stay with me. Showing my credentials as a nurse who had worked overseas for more than ten years went a long way. You know how it is here, anything from London or the US must be top notch. I also mentioned my connections to Doctors Without Borders and promised that I would adhere to all the doctor's prescriptions for my father. They eventually agreed so I drove him home, my father a shadow of his former self. Only the slight glint in his eye assured me that he was still in there. While we were driving he suddenly started laughing.

"How did you do it, Zo Zo?" he chuckled. "What did you tell them to get me out of there?"

He knew exactly who I was. He said that as soon as I left after a visit he would be relieved because he could imagine me being free. He was petrified that they would lock me up too.

"Of course I knew who my own daughter was," he said. "But I wasn't about to let that on. Those people are evil but no amount of medicine would make me ever forget my own daughter." He beat his chest and cackled and we laughed at his sly ways. I realized that if I could spend more time monitoring him, I could help him work through the unprocessed trauma and fear. I adjusted his medication and made sure he ate properly. He had a good appetite and followed all my instructions like he wanted me to know that he trusted me. Some days he was more lucid than others. We crammed in a lot those first few months. I took him to Durban to watch the sea and the joy on his face brought tears to my eyes. I swear, if people on the other side have a way of contacting us they did that day. As we sat there, a school of dolphins came close, squeaking and almost matching the sound of my father's delight. And in case that wasn't enough, the sunlight hit the water in such a way that the waves had a goldish color to them. It was pure magic for me and my father.

I then took him to Moses Mabhida Stadium and he cried when we got into the elevator and went up to the viewing deck. We watched brave youngsters bungee jump and my father whooped for them, throwing his fists up like he just scored a goal in a soccer match. It was fascinating to watch him so childlike in an old man's body. To see his pure delight about the soccer stadium, the sea and the buzz of it all. He loved seeing posters of Zakumi the leopard, the World Cup mascot, so I bought him one of his own. We squashed it in the car and he kept looking back to make sure it was still there.

"Thank you Zo Zo," he said. "This was the best thing for me today and I'm so happy. If this sack of old bones doesn't make it to see that first match, I'll still die a happy man because of today. I know the Grim Reaper is coming, you know."

We drove in silence; my heart was full and I felt sad reflecting on my father's words. I was grateful to have that quiet time and I saw how one day out had made such a difference to him. I'd told him that we had finally won our freedom. He didn't dismiss it and it felt so good to see the happiness in his eyes. He watched people intently and the absence of signs like "Blacks only" and "Europeans only" finally convinced him. At the stadium, I asked a man to walk him to the bathroom and I assured my father that I would wait for him. He was hesitant but he came back and said, "You were right my Zo Zo, we are free. We pee with the rest of them now." He laughed and shook his head like it all made sense. He said most Blacks no longer hung their heads. "There is something loose in their bodies."

I decided to take my father to the Tatham Art Gallery to show him that things really had changed. I chose seats for us on the balcony overlooking the uMgungundlovu City Hall. A tall, young white waitress came to serve us and asked my father what tea he wanted. She took our order and my father's eyes were full of disbelief. He held his mouth and shook his head.

"I never thought I would live to see the day. Huh, Zo Zo. I wouldn't have believed you until I sat here and saw it for myself." He said there were two things that would take some getting used to for him and that was paying a tip and leaving food, like the milk we didn't use for our tea.

We drove home and both slept with content hearts that night. We filled our days with excursions, including one to his old school, which was still standing and operational, and he recognized the soccer pitch immediately. I was nervous he would break down at seeing things from his past but as he continued to show improvement, I took him to the family plot situated behind Wadley Stadium where my mother and Gogo Tu were buried. He knelt in between their headstones and I was shocked when he started reciting the long Eucharist prayers he had once learned by rote. It was word for word from the book that was used at catechism when he was a child. We then sat on a blanket under a tree after his recitation, quiet and still with our thoughts.

He reminisced about his soccer matches at Wadley and how the stadium would fill up and everyone would call him "Jack London" on the pitch. Until the day he broke his ankle and met my mother. His face softened as memories took him back to the days of romance with her.

"It was the most painful injury, Zo Zo. I was howling in that hospital. It was only a few days later when I felt embarrassed about my lack of restraint that I began to notice your mother. When she finally allowed me to drape my arm around her as we walked around together to strengthen my ankle, I milked it for all I could to get into her good books. I cleaned up my unfinished business with other women because I knew instantly that she was the one for me. It was a good time in our lives and look what she left me with," he smiled and pinched my cheek.

$$\equiv$$

On Human Right's Day, March 21, I buried my dad. We had gone to sleep without any indication that anything was wrong, but he just didn't wake up and had passed peacefully in his sleep. I woke up alone. He was laid to rest with dignity next to my mother and Gogo Tu. My heart was full and I was so glad I had followed my instinct to move back and be with him during those last few months. I was so blessed to have had him as my father. He had broken the curse of incest in my mother's family and was a good solid man who operated with love to love away my mother's family stain. It takes a loving man to remove the stains of other men, expanding the hearts of the women they choose to love with all their imperfections.

Of course I was sad, but the three months I had spent with him gave me so much. He became my medicine and I felt so relieved that all the guilt I had carried with me while exploring the world had been unnecessary. My father saw me as a bird that needed to fly but he knew I would always find my way home. I felt lighter at his funeral and when we sang, I felt a burden lift from my shoulders. I was alone but I felt surrounded by so much love.

My father must have been looking down on me knowing I needed closure in other parts of my life because as the mourners were filing out the church offering me their condolences, Sindi walked up to me. The shock of seeing her took my breath away and all the grudges I held against her and Freedom for all those years melted away. She took my hand like she did at Bhoyi's funeral and held it, steadying me. She had heard that I was back in the country but work had kept her from seeing me sooner so when she found out about my father's death, she dropped everything and flew from Johannesburg to see me. She had to fly back right away but she promised to return and that we would watch the opening match of the World Cup at Gogo Tu's house together.

We chatted on the phone over the next few months and the conversations were awkward. Time had done so much damage but I needed to hear everything from her face to face. Only then could we try mend what time and misunderstanding had done to us. She was the only one who could fill in the gaps for me. Bhoyi was gone, of course, and I didn't know if Freedom was even still alive. It was so good to have finally found someone I had prayed for and looked for all those years during my travels.

$$\equiv$$

Sindi arrived at Gogo Tu's house just like we planned. She brought her daughter with her, a pretty teenager about the same age as our country's democracy. She had named her Zoe, after me. I squeezed her tight and she told me she was happy to finally meet me after all the stories she'd heard about me from her mom. Little Zoe helped ease a lot of the initial awkwardness between me and Sindi. We cooked a feast together and watched the opening ceremony of the World Cup. It felt so fitting that our team scored the opening goal. When Siphiwe Tshabalala scored that goal against Mexico, we all ran outside and let the sound of the vuvuzelas from Caluza wash over us. We had come full circle. We screamed and laughed and cried.

"You missed it by three months," I said softly to myself, thinking of my father as a hadeda squawked and flew out from the tree we were standing under.

It felt good not to be alone and I felt like I had found a part of my family. Sindi was beautiful and so dignified. The softness she had when we were young was gone and replaced with the confidence of someone who has come into their own. Maybe it had to do with being a mother but it was obvious that she knew how to look after herself. Little Zoe told me that her mother sometimes behaved like she was still in uMkhonto weSizwe. She had workout routines that were regimented without deviations. It was the same with the vocal workouts to keep her singing voice in top shape and when driving she routinely checked the rear-view mirror to check that no one was tailing her. And she was completely over the top with the safety measures for Zoe. They had a beautiful mother-daughter bond that made me feel like I had missed out on something special with my mom.

We were all tired and retired early that night. I was stalling, though; I didn't know how much I actually wanted to hear about what happened all those years ago. The pain of Sindi and Freedom leaving me behind that night felt as strong as ever. There were times when the pain didn't feel too bad but it was a physical ache that I knew I needed to work through and I could only do that by talking to Sindi.

$$\equiv$$

"Zo, I can't go to sleep until I tell you what happened that night." I heard Sindi's voice behind me and I turned and saw she was standing in my doorway. She came into my room and sat on the bed and I felt the grief engulf me. She let me cry and sat quietly next to me. I felt raw inside and like I was waiting for the signal all over again.

"How could you, Sindi? How could you leave me? I was the one who waited until *you* were ready and then I was the one who got left behind!"

She remained silent until she felt it was safe to talk. She handed me a glass of water. She was so assured and had dealt with many meltdowns in her career. It was slightly unnerving, like she had an on-off switch.

"Zo, you were marked. Someone snitched to the Boers, to that security agent Stoney and his mellow-yellow dogs. They didn't have all the information but they speculated that since you and Bhoyi were involved you would skip the country after his burial. Freedom saw the van that night and we dived into the mealies on the side of the road to avoid being seen by the lights of Stoney's van. We crawled until we reached the school and then ran along the side of the Mphelandaba mountains. We crossed the uMsunduzi and then Freedom stopped and held me by my shoulders. His eyes burning he said, 'Listen to me, Sindi. We are doing this and it's not going to be easy.' He handed me a tiny silver pistol and told me to use it to defend myself. 'No hesitation. You point and shoot and if we get caught and you can't get to the pistol, use your hands. Stick your fingers in eyes and then push with everything you have. If it's a Boer, aim for the nose and push their sharp nose upwards towards their brain.' He demonstrated the maneuver. 'Remember what Bhoyi said, we would not die idling, okay?' We carried on and got to the Edendale YMCA just as the comrades were being loaded up for Swaziland."

That's when I remembered that I kept seeing flashlights that night and had known better than to go outside to see who it was. We had agreed on a whistle so I ignored the lights. Inkatha sleepers would have made a meal out of a teenage girl like me. Now I realized it was Stoney and his dogs. I searched Sindi's eyes and she looked back intensely, her eyes full of the untold horror of that night.

"Zo, I cried all the way to Swaziland. I was so afraid. It was happening so fast and there was no turning back. I couldn't think of home so I blocked it all out. Some days we were hidden in safe houses and felt human, while others we slept out in the open and felt like animals. I called myself Mathapelo Blacks so even if you tried to find me, you wouldn't have been able to. I embraced that name, I became it. My every move was a prayer and it was drilled into me so much that it took me time to fully respond to my real name eventually. Zo, I'm so tired, friend. Let me tell you everything after a good night's rest. You have to believe me though when I say you were marked."

I believed her and I felt stupid for ever thinking that they left me behind on purpose. It had been enough for one day so we both decided to try and get some rest. I hardly slept as my mind was racing, linking the gaps of my past and the fork in the road we had now been granted. My heart was overflowing to have come full circle with my friend.

$$\equiv$$

We woke up the next morning feeling drained but we also felt cleansed of something. Little Zoe surprised me by knowing her way around the kitchen and made a breakfast spread of oats, pancakes, bacon and eggs. We drank tea and chatted. Sindi said it was boarding school that taught her daughter how to be independent. She had made sure that Zoe grew up in Pietermaritzburg and she sent her to Wykeham Collegiate as a boarder. She wanted her daughter to have a grounded and wholesome upbringing in a small idyllic environment, as opposed to a fast-paced city like Johannesburg. I could see Sindi was proud of Zoe but there was something else that she wasn't telling me. And then I saw it. Zoe looked like Freedom. She was Freedom's child! When I realized, I spilled my tea.

Sindi nodded and smiled and told me it was a long story for adults only and that she'd tell me after dropping Zoe off at a friend's house for the weekend. Zoe told her mom that she would be safe before Sindi could even ask. She knew her mother's tick about safety and jokingly called her "OCD" behind her back.

Once we got back from dropping Zoe off, we carried on the conversation from the night before. Sindi told me that for the first two years after skipping the border she knew the kind of fear that she wouldn't wish on anyone, not even on the Boer that killed Bhoyi.

"It was so frightening, Zo. If I wasn't dodging venomous snakes in the bushes where we camped, I was dodging the Boers' bullets and if it wasn't the Boers' bullets, it was their penises. They raped their political prisoners, men or women, with impunity. And if it wasn't the Boers' penises, it was the spies who were snitching on us. You couldn't trust anything or anyone. In the senselessness of war, I couldn't even fully trust Freedom. We learned quickly to pretend we didn't know each other and we all treated each other like we were dealing with double agents. Not everyone was there for the right reasons. Attachment was a weakness and the enemy could break you by inflicting pain on the ones they knew you cared about. Most infuriating for me was dodging my own comrades' or the commanders' penises. They were just as notorious as the Boers, especially when you rejected their advances and I had to stop acting coy very fast so that I could protect myself. I developed a sixth sense about anybody I was around and I made it clear that I was there for my country not to be a fuck toy for anybody."

I remind Sindi about when we were kids and Gogo Tu used to tell us to listen to the voice inside us. Sindi tells me she often remembered that and had been grateful so many times that she listened to that voice inside her. Gogo Tu used to say she was giving us intuition as a "compass." It was Sindi, Bhoyi and me. The Three Musketeers before we knew Freedom. We must have all been about six or seven at the time when Gogo Tu sat us down and told us to count to ten in our heads. When we were done, she said the voice inside us that was counting without saying the words out loud was the real us. We must have looked confused so she said it was like looking in the mirror for the first time and knowing it is you being reflected back at you without being told. Sindi said that sometimes the voice was mean to her and said hurtful things, like she was stupid. Gogo Tu said that was a good observation and it would get confusing as we got older because there would be many voices and they would be loud and sometimes urgent, telling us to go in different directions. She said to pay attention only to the steady, quiet voice and we would never go wrong. That it is the voice that can never be tainted or touched by the madness of the world.

"Zo, I listened to my voice all those years thanks to Gogo Tu and I believe it is the reason I am alive today. I eventually got myself out of the bush without having to open my legs. I had looked and felt like prey out there so I fought for my life. I learned early on to pick up the 'look' and I called it out openly. The boys preferred to catch their prey unaware. I didn't play the seduction game but I was cornered once while bathing in the river. They didn't catch me that day, thanks to Genevieve. She was a hell of a comrade who came from Cape Town and, after escaping one too many of these sexual raids, Genevieve and I decided to watch over each other. She would stand on top of the hill and scan the area while I bathed and then I did the same for her. Genevieve was on edge because she had overheard the others making plans. She suggested we skip bathing that day but I couldn't because menstruation was making me feel like fetid human garbage. I needed to be clean and, with my hormones raging, I was fuming that I didn't have the basic human right to clean my body because I was scared of the people I was fighting alongside it for.

"We defiantly went down to the river that day and Genevieve stayed hidden while I bathed and she kept watch. She had saved us all from an attack of SADF soldiers once after convincing our commander that we should all sleep in the field instead of the house we were allocated in Swaziland during our first few days there. There was a long debate until we all filed out of the warm safe house that actually had beds in it but she was insistent that something was wrong. I am so glad the commander listened because at two o'clock the next morning we watched from the field of overgrown mealies as the SADF soldiers surrounded the house. I was shaking like a leaf and grateful their sniffer dogs were not with them otherwise they would have sniffed us out. Genevieve saved all of us that day.

"Just as I was drying myself off that day, I heard Genevieve's raspy voice shout, 'Run Ma se kind, run.' I froze and Genevieve shot a round from her rifle into the air and I was shocked out of my temporary paralysis. We ran up the hill back to the camp. I was kaalgat naked and on my period and I was furious. Genevieve and I made such a stink but nothing was done. In fact, they threatened to report Genevieve for wasteful use of a rifle. Things came to a head and she didn't take that accusation lying down. Her rage was a wonder to watch and nobody could shut her up. 'I came to fight for my rights, not to fend off my own brothers. At home I was fending off my own father and had to skip the border. Where is a woman's place in this world if we can't be safe at home or with our fellow comrades? I might as well sommer put this bullet through my head.'

"We all jumped her and wrestled the rifle away from her. She was howling and there was a hushed silence throughout the camp. Boys were ashamed of themselves and started murmuring. Then the ones who coped by clowning around started to laugh at our river escapade and my nudity. I was the laughing stock but rather that than be violated. The commander didn't know what to do about our insistence that our comrades should be charged. Instead of doing something, he moved me to the cultural activists group, together with most of the children of the high-ranking commanders. I was starting to tell visiting leadership that the women in the camps were not being treated well and soon thereafter I was taken out and flown to Holland where a lot of exiles were being sent at the time.

"Genevieve is one of the few comrades I have respect for. Don't be fooled when some comrades act like they were the only ones in the struggle. I was surprised by the number of colored comrades who were in the trenches with us. There were three types of women in the camps: the older more established women, others who were prepared to be used, and those who ended up putting a bullet in their heads from betrayal and frustration. It was crushing to be there and to realize you were not safe among your own. I didn't miss a single one of those other comrades' stinky asses, not even the women who attached themselves to certain men for protection. I couldn't have done that even if I wanted to because Freedom was shipped off to Russia after proving himself proficient in weapons. If push came to shove, I would have chosen Freedom because of our personal history; he had planted a bull's-eye on that Boer who killed Bhoyi, after all. News of his reputation traveled and the day he left the camp, it took everything in me not to break down. Seeing him climb into that truck, it felt like my knees were going to give in under me. He searched all of our faces and found mine in the crowd and said, 'For Bhoyi, comrade long live.' I smiled weakly and he squared his jaw and quickly looked away.

"The next time I saw Freedom was a decade later in London. He was already back in South Africa with the transition team working on integrating the military forces from SADF to SANDF and he was in London for a mission he was vague about. I had to laugh; they had trained him well. I was in London to perform with the band I was in from Holland. I had worked myself out of hard politics by then and was into the arts, specializing in jazz vocals. I had redone Nina Simone's "Mississippi Goddamn" to "South Africa Goddamn" and I never finished my set without playing Billie Holiday's "Strange Fruit." That song takes me back to the day Bhoyi died in front of my eyes and I never manage to finish it without bawling. My stage name was Ms. B and music saved me back then. The camps had left me disillusioned and were places where women, especially pretty young ones like me, were nothing.

"When I saw Freedom that day in London he apologized, but I reminded him that we were all there for a purpose. He interrupted me and said he was sorry about what he had said at Bhoyi's funeral that day. About how angry he was and for saying we wouldn't ever overcome things in our lives.

"He remembered that I sang 'We Shall Overcome' so convincingly that day that it had made him think we could overcome things. He said it felt like it was lulling all of us into a false sense of hope. But there we were, years later and we *had* overcome it. He told me I had been right all along and that music was my gift and had become my ticket out.

"Zo, I don't know if it was the red wine that night or the exhilarating feeling that we were finally getting our

South Africa back or sitting across from an old friend I had skipped the country with, but I felt alright for the first time in a long while. I felt safe enough to spend the night in his hotel room and it felt like it was the most natural thing. We talked through the night and the next day until we had to part ways because I was performing and he was wrapping up his mystery project and heading home. It never crossed either of our minds that little Zoe would decide to choose us as her parents. I was preparing to come home anyway to cast my vote when I found out I was pregnant. After voting, I kept my alias, Mathapelo Blacks. I settled in Cape Town, putting distance between me and the past and I found Freedom to tell him the result of sipping warm wine that night in that cold city. He was as shocked as I had been. He often visited from Pretoria to make sure I was okay but we never talked about us, it was mostly about the baby I was carrying. We would be like a couple when he spent the night but then nothing was ever said the next day. I desperately wanted to hear how he felt but I found out much later that he was afraid I would reject him if he told me the truth. He told me I was the one thing he wanted the most when we were at school and when Bhoyi stole me from him, it killed him inside.

"I found this all out much later once he had been sworn in as Minister of Education and married his Boer PA, Hannetjie. I was torn apart Zo, torn apart. Only then did I realize that I was in love with him. That the woman he chose to settle down with was a Boer felt like a knife cutting through my heart. Even he seemed uncomfortable every time I exclaimed about his Boer wife. My baby was three years old by then and there were no more ambiguous overnight stays now that he was a married man. I told him he was welcome to see his daughter anytime but there was nothing more between us. We felt stupid after confessing how much we had loved each other and it felt like we wasted so much. It all took some adjustment and if anyone had told me that I would be a single mother and a jazz singer who hated politics, I would have laughed at them!

"Little Zoe was five when Freedom came for a visit one night, drunk out of his mind. He flopped onto the sofa and cried himself to sleep and woke up sheepishly the next day and told me that his wife had cancer. He cried openly in front of us and left, promising to send us tickets for Zoe's birthday to fly to Pretoria. True to his word, he did and little Zoe was beside herself with excitement. But then Zo, I nearly lost my child when we were there. I shudder every time I think about it. We went out for a meal together when a giant of a policeman came out of nowhere and tried to attack Freedom. I couldn't really work out what was happening but the gist of it was that the man was Freedom's brother-in-law and he was convinced that Freedom was cheating on his sister. His monstrous fist landed on my child and knocked her out. I spent weeks in the ICU waiting for little Zoe to come out of her coma. I had to move up to Joburg and she eventually recovered and it worked out well because her dad was nearby to do the co-parenting thing.

"Eventually Freedom and I agreed that a boarding school in our home town of Pietermaritzburg would be a perfect place for Zoe to blossom. It was a win-win for all of us. And so here we are, Zo Zo, that's the story of my life after all those years of running and dodging."

≡

"It was surreal, Mkhulu, and for a while Sindi and I just sat there digesting the madness of our lives. I did a lot of laughing and crying. I finally put down the heavy load that I had been carrying all those years of feeling that I had been betrayed by Sindi and Freedom. I became an auntie to their wonderful daughter, my namesake, and felt like I had something close to family in my life. Or chosen family at least, and that grounded me. Little Zoe would spend her weekend pass with me since I was a short ride away from Wykeham. Sindi and I shared our first love and then shared a daughter who made us both so proud and our hearts full."

MADALA

THE SILENCE BETWEEN us is long and I'm reeling because, of course, I know the story of that minister punched by my colleague, Jakob Greyling. I wasn't shocked to hear about the camps and how they treated women but, while I'd heard things, I didn't know they were so awful. I suppose there is no logic to war. We did the same in the army to any captured rebels we could lay our hands on. It reminded me of what Miles Davis said in his biography that an erect penis has no conscience. I'm ashamed to say he was right. I know what we did in the name of supposedly protecting our country and we justified all manner of evil. Any war-torn country carries unmentionable pain and humiliation inflicted on its women. The irony is that I recognized myself in many of those bastards. I used to do those things to women and I particularly hated women who put up a fight. A part of me prays that I die before I have to tell my Girlie that part of my story.

All the talk about this virus and possible lockdown leaves me hoping that I contract the damn thing and exit this world before I have to face anything more about my past. I know that's a terrible thing to wish for but the links between our stories are adding to the weight of the bricks I am going to drop on Zoe with my story. She's going to think I am a monster. Especially because I'm playing the role of a grandfather, something I haven't got to do with my own biological grandchildren. At times I can sense Zoe's hesitation but I'm in too deep now not to probe any further. I know to give her time to decide what layer of her story she wants to peel away next.

I wasn't surprised to hear how the comrades loved their jazz music. We used to sit in our vans listening in on the houses we were targeting. We had them wired so we could eavesdrop to pick up any information on what was being planned. In some of those houses all we heard were the tunes of Nina Simone damning the whole state or the mourning sound of Billie Holiday detailing the gruesome lynching of Black men hanging from trees like strange fruits. Some days when things were really bad, we would intercept night vigils where women were singing and praying. As they tired, the haunting voice of Mahalia Jackson and her "God's Gonna Separate the Wheat from the Tares" sent ice into my stomach each time I heard her sing.

Something about dodging bullets and eluding death made many of our targets party hard too when they felt they had the chance to let loose. We intercepted weddings and listened in to what I imagine was true love made whole through laughter and declarations, women promising to wait and men promising to protect. I don't know if any of these sacred rites touched any of my men but if they did they dared not show it. It wasn't said but we all knew we were no match for some of the music and its ability to move us.

The saxophone wizard, Miles Davis, put us all into a trance and we'd forget all about our mission. There is something to be said about the power of music. The times we would leave with nothing to report back, we'd have to make things up to avoid being seen as useless but we would be full from the music. The comrades' taste in music showed me that we weren't dealing with fools. There was something sophisticated that I didn't associate with the caricatures we had been indoctrinated to believe. They were more than just people who served us tea, tended our gardens and looked after our children. Despite my hate back then, jazz music reached me and yanked the wall of hate I had built up. That's how I got to read all about the genius that was Miles. The funny thing is that if we had met back in the bad old days, it would have been two bulls clashing and it would have been bloody. I have no doubt he was his own man who didn't play by the rules of any man. His saxophone won in the end.

$$\equiv$$

I must have zoned out and dozed off because when I wake up, Zoe is long gone, having tucked me in for the night.

ZOE

THE NEXT DAY I'm back with Mkhulu and he asks me more questions and urges me to continue with my story.

I tell him how I fell in love and got pregnant in London just like Sindi and how funny it was when we realized that we both conceived our children there. I fell for a green-eyed Irish drunk who concealed his drinking problem well at first but I soon caught on. I'd been there a little over a year and was working at Cromwell Hospital. It wasn't as hectic as Edendale but at least we didn't have to deal with war-like situations. People in London were dying slowly from their lifestyles; young ones came in with alcohol poisoning and botched suicides and the old ones had diseases like diabetes, cancer and Alzheimer's. Occasionally we had a girl come in with a botched genital mutilation from a fanatical immigrant family and those cases shocked me to my core. The girls were dead inside from the pain.

Our nursing force was a United Nations of women from all over the world; from African countries, Ukraine, Poland, Greece, India, Spain and Mexico. We all stayed in a boarding house in Earl's Court across from a pub called The Black Bird. It was fun and distracting enough for me to forget home and immerse myself in the museums and galleries that I went to on my days off, despite the constant drizzle and damp weather. The summers were pleasant and I got along with most of the girls.

Spring was in the air the day I met Aidan O'Neill at The Black Bird. He came in with his rowdy group of friends to celebrate St. Patrick's Day. I remember everything was green, even the mashed potatoes with our bangers, and Ameera, a gregarious Muslim girl from Jordan, swore us to secrecy for committing a mortal haram by eating pork. We overheard Aidan's friends daring him to come and talk to me and the next thing he stood up and came over to our table.

He whispered in my ear that his friends had dared him to ask me for a dance, an Irish jig, and feverishly said to me, "Please, please Ms., don't say no. I'd never hear the end of it if you reject me. Humor me, will ya?" I took his hand and walked with him to the dance floor and the boys roared and cheered. He was as pleased as punch. I think the green ale had gotten to me too but he had beautiful green eyes and long black hair tied in a ponytail. He guided me through the dance steps and, once the song was over, he kissed my hand and I went back to the girls. He sent another glass of ale to the table with a note that said, *Thank you for helping me save face in front of my friends. Please can I have your number, Ms.? I'd love to dance with you again.*

I drank the ale but stalled on giving him my number. The girls were just as rowdy as the guys and teased me the rest of the night about a budding romance between us. We left without giving Aidan my number but he must have seen us filing into our boarding house opposite the pub because the next morning we woke up and all had a note slid underneath our doors. *This is for the tall African girl I danced with last night. My name is Aidan O'Neill and I'd really like to see her again. Ms., please, please, please call me.* He had written his number on each note. The giddy and hungover girls gathered at my door, holding their notes, and said it was such a romantic gesture that I should call him.

I called Aidan two days later and we met up that evening. We walked to Speaker's Corner in Hyde Park, we talked about St. Patrick's Day at The Black Bird and laughed about his friends. "They couldn't believe I actually did it," he told me. "But I never told them how I groveled in your ear!"

Aidan was an artisan who built fiddles, mandolins and banjos, a skill he had learned from his grandpa. He loved talking about his work but his parents had pushed him to study so he had studied literature focusing on South American and African writers. It's ironic that most of the African writers I read after that were recommended by an Irishman! He told me about the Irish writer Frank McCourt and his book *Angela's Ashes*. I loved that book and Aidan was so happy that that he got me a copy of McCourt's second book *'tis*, which I also enjoyed.

We were inseparable from then on and explored London together. He was like a personal tour guide because he knew so much about the history of places we were sightseeing.

But his friends started to resent me just as my father's did when he met my mother. Aidan hardly saw them and they felt slighted and like they had been dumped. Sometimes we hung out with a few of them who were nice to me, but some of them stared at me like I was an oddity and their conversations were awkward when I was around. One of them had a habit of calling me "Black Bird" and I refused to let that name stick. He never hung out with us again and I was relieved because there was something about him that reminded me of the Boers back home.

Aidan came back to South Africa with me for the New Year celebration at the end of 1999. He said that if the world changed like everyone said it was going to, he wanted to be with me in Africa. I fell pregnant five years into our relationship. I never met his family and he would go to Ireland alone, but that suited me. He told me it would take some getting used to for them to accept that he was dating an African woman. The pregnancy ended up being our undoing. At first I thought it was just bad morning sickness but I soon started to feel like I was falling apart. I didn't know how to express it but something was amiss. I wasn't well but it was in a way I couldn't explain. I'd go to bed feeling uneasy and wake up naar and feeling like I hadn't slept.

Five months into the pregnancy, I was traveling on the tube to meet Aidan. I sat next to a huge Sudanese old man whose skin was blue-black with fearsome warrior scarring on his forehead. He smiled at me and we exchanged pleasantries, which was kind of a taboo thing to do on the tube, but it was familiar to me and reminded me of home.

I smiled weakly and was feeling very unwell by the time we reached Piccadilly Circus. As I stood up, I felt a rush of warmth between my legs and there was blood all over my white pants. The old man saw what had happened and swiftly took off his large scarf to cover me and helped me off the tube, guiding me to a seat at the station.

Seeing my embarrassment, he said, "You have nothing to worry about, young one, I am old and I have seen it all. I have my own daughters so think of me as your father. Now, who can I call for you?"

I gave him Aidan's number and felt too weak to even cry. I felt woozy and sat waiting for Aidan and burst into tears when I saw him walking towards me. They took me to the hospital where the doctor confirmed my miscarriage. I never saw the old man again but I will never forget his kindness and warmth. He had insisted on coming to the hospital with us but after I was taken in I never saw him again.

Aidan was crushed and sat by my bed and cried with me for our unborn baby. Once I was released from the hospital something was broken between us and he drank himself into a stupor. All the demons I had tried to outrun came for me in my dreams and I'd wake up drenched in sweat. My heart felt bruised like when I was left behind all those years ago. The hospital gave me time off and the girls were very supportive. They made me wonderful food and chased Aidan away when I couldn't deal with his drunken babble. I was broken. I thought of coming home but I had no one to come home to. My last visit to see my father had been so upsetting. Things got worse and it hurt to breathe. There was nothing wrong with my lungs and it wasn't something the doctors could pinpoint but the act itself of inhaling and exhaling was painful. I was drowning inside and my dreams were so vivid that I sometimes thought I could hear the cries of the baby I had lost. Other times I'd see my friends' grey corpses riddled with bullet holes.

One day I woke up feeling clear-headed and I decided to break up with Aidan. We cried together and he left London to start over back home in Ireland. Before the drink got hold of him, Aidan was a light spirit and loving man and I would always care about him.

I started writing poetry and sent some poems to a few newspapers. The feedback was positive and the local newspaper published some of them. Aidan had sparked something in me and I poured all my pain into writing and slowly started feeling stronger. The poems were mostly musings of home and nostalgia-driven but it turned out many South Africans in the expat community related to them. The editor then asked for 800-word pieces about my travels or the new democracy in South Africa and so my writing career began.

I went back to work at the hospital but seven days in and London blew up in a series of coordinated bombings. It felt like I was back at Edendale Hospital. There was a cacophony of ambulances delivering mangled bodies and we worked long hours. I thrived in it and it distracted me from thinking about anything, especially Aidan. I continued writing whenever I had spare time.

It was during this period that our hospital acquired more nurses and doctors on its staff. Kyle Botham was one of the student doctors who joined the hospital. He constantly triggered me with his arrogance and condescending tone, but I didn't pick up on it at first as he seemed charming. None of us could place his posh accent as it faltered between British and Australian. He sat with us on his breaks, made jokes and asked about our home countries. He heard from some of the excitable girls who were vying for his attention that I was from South Africa and that my writing was being published in the paper. He'd read the pieces and pass comments like "Oh bless" in the most nauseatingly patronizing way, and because I was still finding my feet in my writing I felt insecure. Bullies have a nose for these things. He'd point out mistakes; the odd typo here or a grammatical inconsistency there and make comments about journalism "going to the dogs."

He'd shake his head sympathetically as I sheepishly hung my head in shame. Satisfaction would fill his eyes when he knew his knife was in deep. I had learned enough to know not to argue or call him out and I tried to ignore him. I'd end up with a headache and him smacking in his signature smugness. I couldn't give him the satisfaction of insulting me further and tried to keep my distance. I would watch him out of the corner of my eye and observe him looking at me closely to see if I was taking the bait. It was sickening to feel shredded by somebody like that and at first it frightened me and slowed down my writing process, but then something else took over and it motivated me to keep writing.

One night later that year, it had been a long night in the ER and we had lost a few people. The emotion was thick in the air. At one point, a few of us were sitting in the staffroom when Kyle walked in crying. He had lost a little five-year-old girl. What he then said was picked up by no one else but I knew it immediately. That fucker was no Englishman, he was a platteland boy. I walked out quietly while the girls comforted him. Bliksem. I'd recognize that word anywhere.

I then did some digging and I found out that the bastard was a graduate of Wits University. It all clicked into place for me because from what I had heard, whites were no longer having it good back home. They were calling it "reverse racism" so he must have hated bumping into me in London, plus seeing my writing about South Africa in the newspaper. I was resolute that I was going to write even more about what had been done to the Blacks and what had been stolen from us. I applied the tactics of a wolf and kept my distance but was never not watchful of him. I knew when I had got to him. He was livid when he read the piece and I had obviously stabbed the soft spot. The writing disputed reverse racism and the fallacy of the rainbow nation and I knew then that my job was done. I stopped playing silly games and focused earnestly on my writing.

I was being commissioned for more and more pieces so when I got a call to meet up with journalists from other countries touring the BBC and St. Bride's Church—the Journalists' Church in Fleet Street—I readily agreed. The touring group was affiliated with Cardiff University in Wales and I was asked to give a talk about how I landed in London mixing writing and nursing.

After that, things snowballed and I got a call from a travel journalist who was going to be visiting southern Africa.

He wanted to avoid the touristy spots and experience the "real" Africa. He thought it would be perfect if I accompanied him because he would do the broadcasting and I would do the writing. He had planned the trip for the second half of the following year and the money he offered was incredible.

It sealed the deal for me and I tendered my resignation in good time to wrap things up in London. Whatever happened after that, I would deal with. I felt myself let out a sigh of relief and before I knew it I was hot-footing it out of Cromwell having served a decade there.

The first six months of traveling through the townships of South Africa, Namibia, Mozambique, Zambia, Zimbabwe, Botswana and Lesotho were some of the best times of my life. It also gave me an idea and I decided to work six-month contracts in the South African health services and then travel for the other six months of the year. I'd blog about my experiences and sell my writing to news outlets. It all fell into place quite easily and I hardly thought about what could go wrong. So much had gone wrong in my life and I was still in one piece so I figured that whatever fell apart would correct itself and so I left it at that.

$$\equiv$$

"So here we are, Mkhulu, my second decade of working as a renegade and I haven't starved yet, how about that, huh?"

MADALA

IT'S APRIL AND the weather has changed. It's nippy outside and the country is now in full lockdown mode. My Girlie has moved into the premises of the home and is locked down with us as an essential worker. I am happy she decided to stay. We're drinking a lot of hot chocolate, not only out of habit but because it's getting cold at night. We spend hours talking. The news is more like the movies than reality and our president is looking frightened and tired. Our health minister keeps us informed of the increasing numbers of cases and tries to give us assurances, as does our minister of police. Drunks and smokers are not amused by the ban on alcohol and cigarettes. Ms. Rajah addresses all of us oldies, reminding us to stay calm. She's introduced an hour of calming music in the morning and the evening.

=

I have decided that best way to unfold the rest of my story to my Girlie is through an album of photos that I hand to her one morning. In the first photograph, my ma, Anneke, is sitting on a rock, looking straight at the camera with a tiny smile forming at the corners of her mouth. Her eyes play a trick on me because it feels like she is looking at me and that she knows every godawful, deep, shameful secret of mine but she loves me anyway. Don't the dead have a vantage point to observe all our foolishness?

"This is my ma, my Girlie. I never got to meet her but from what I was told about her, I feel like she was the right mother for me and I was the right son for her."

My birth, when Kristina told me about it, always left me feeling like I had done a terrible thing even before I was born. Kristina wasn't one to shelter the youth; she spoke to children like she would to adults. My Oumagrootjie and Kristina were my mothers. Oumagrootjie was the owner of the farm, Groot Dame, the Great Lady, and Kristina lived on the farm. They felt like one person to me. Two servings of mothering was both good and bad. Most children only have one mother so if they're naughty they get one scolding and if they are good, they get one dose of love. I, on the other hand, got two dollops of scolding, which was bad if you knew those two fearsome women, but I also got two doses of love when I did things well. It was the best time for me when I got hard candies, sticky toffees and cotton candy. It left me grinning and daydreaming about my own world.

The details of my birth were sketchy as Oumagrootjie was not much of a talker and saved her words for when it was absolutely necessary. That was until I found some of her writing and the details of my birth were not the only things I found out. I also got to understand the hell she had had to deal with in her life and the courage she used to protect the Groot Dame. Come to think of it, my survival skill of "'n boer maak 'n plan" was inherited from her.

What little Kristina did tell me about my birth left me convinced that I had killed my ma. She would be horrified if she knew that her reticence to speak about Ma left me damaged for the rest of my life. Guilt was a thorn in my side when I began to understand what it meant to be dead and added to this was the fact that I was a bit of a loskop as a boy. Sometimes I would be on top of the world and the next I would be picking fights. Other times I would be so down in the dumps that I would be frightened to leave the farm and go to school.

Kristina was a medicine woman, a midwife and a hell of a cook. What I didn't realize then, but what I can now add to her long list of talents, was that she could spin a tale so vividly that you found yourself in the story, seeing and feeling the details. A story is about the details and the benefit of hindsight. Time stood still when Kristina painted a picture with her words. If you were sensitive, it was best not to listen to her stories before you went to bed because you would be sure not to sleep.

According to Kristina, it was as if I was refusing to be born that day. It was 1939 and the country was throwing in its lot with England and declaring war on the Germans. For hours, I clung to the walls of my mother's womb, refusing to come out, and causing her indescribable pain.

"Breathe Anneke, breathe," Oumagrootjie instructed,

helping usher me into this maddeningly beautiful world. Ma was breathing and screaming at different intervals, sweating and blistering red in the face, fighting to get me out. I was fighting my own battle to stay where I was while my pa was in another room in the house, jittery and pacing, making sure he was in earshot.

Oumagrootjie then called out to my pa, Adriaan van Rooyen, and told him to fetch Kristina because my ma was having a breech birth. My pa took off in the direction of the farmworkers' compound to call Kristina to come and help Oumagrootjie, the Matriarch. That's what they used to call her. Many children on the farm fell from their mother's warm watery place into the two women's hands, screaming blue murder and looking like shrunken and slimy little prunes. Kristina and Oumagrootjie had worked together many times delivering babies and, in some instances, when a cow was in distress, they had delivered calves.

Kristina said she had been expecting to hear from Oumagrootjie because not only did she not like the look of my ma towards the end of her pregnancy, but she'd had a terrible dream and the sight of my pa sent cold shivers down her spine. She said she felt it before it happened and she outran my pa to get to the farmhouse. She launched herself on the floor next to where the Matriarch was kneeling over a groaning Anneke, but she couldn't look her in the eye.

"Merciful Mvelingqangi. What can we say, us mere mortals? If it is written in your books that your will be done, we can only ask at least to save the child. Allow us that, Lord. We have looked after many and we will look after this one too."

The women had communicated with each other without any words but the day I was born the Matriarch was blindsided. When it dawned on her that Kristina meant that she had foreseen something awful, she suddenly stilled and glared at her, willing her to look her in the eyes so she could see the story for herself. Kristina evaded her until finally she had to look at her. She loved my mother so it was with glassy eyes and a crestfallen face that she indicated to the Matriarch, by a slight shake of her head, almost as if she was admitting defeat, that there was something bigger at play. The Matriarch was not big on emotion, but that day she let the pain rip her open and she bellowed like an animal, ran outside and retched.

My ma was whimpering at this point as Kristina kneaded her tummy, maneuvering my breeched body to come out head first. She knew there was no time to waste and that the baby had to come out, so she worked on her stomach until I finally came out, my tiny fists clenched. She said it was like I was disgusted at being disturbed.

My ma finally let out a sigh of relief and said, "Tell Adriaan I love him. Name my baby Hans and tell him how much his ma loves him. Tell him I will be nearby all the days of his life." She fixed me with a loving stare and a smile as she took her last breath.

In the following weeks, Kristina said she took to the task of looking after me and trying to shake the Matriarch out of her grief. It was a hell of a thing and I think losing my ma was one too many heartbreaks and losses for the Matriarch. It was like being back in the war again.

Kristina practically became my mother from them on and even today when a Black woman fixes me with that no-nonsense stare, I feel my old balls jump up and shrink. She didn't suffer fools gladly but balanced it with love when needed. I wasn't the only one who got a firm shake-up from her though; Oumagrootjie received her fair share of tongue-lashings from Kristina too.

On good days, Oumagrootjie would sit and recall stories from her life, but by the time I was a teenager she was in her eighties and practically mute. Kristina, who was in her sixties, kept the stories going. When she told me about the day of my birth she recalled how my pa looked like an orphan standing there, lost.

Children without parents are called orphans and often pitied and shown compassion for the pain of being all alone in the world. But what of the expectant fathers waiting to be fully initiated into manhood, their seed fully planted and breaking into life, and that seed rips open their partner and in the battle of birth fate intervenes? This was what Kristina was thinking when she saw the light leave the blue eyes of my poor father when he worked out that his wife didn't make it.

Soon after I was born, my pa packed his bags and attempted the impossible; he tried to outrun his pain by enlisting in the army. He didn't hate me, the child who had caused the death of the one person he loved more than anything in the world, who triggered something that felt like life in his otherwise numb self, but nothing made sense to him without his wife. Initially, he would offer to relieve Kristina from my cries and fussing, but every time he held me it was like he had stung me and I would cry inconsolably, turning beet red.

"Ubovu wemfan ufana nekhandlela," sang Kristina, soothing me to sleep.

Pa debated whether to stay and try look after me himself, to learn to love it. To do what women did day in and day out. But he was no woman and the possibility of mastering the level of self-sacrifice he had watched women throw themselves into was downright frightening to him. So he chose the war. There was something familiar and fitting there. War called him, it baited him with the possibility of being a stranger among many and fighting anonymous strangers also driven by their own unshed tears and unexpressed emotions. Truth be told, he was slightly relieved to leave behind his monotonous, tragic life.

So it was down to Kristina and Oumagrootjie to raise another child. Two legendary women who survived the British khakis during the South African War. So many of their stories were buried and the truth of what happened during those times was inconvenient, especially in the presence of Black dames like Kristina. Those who didn't write things down never counted for much in history. Oumagrootjie's habit of keeping such detailed diaries makes me want to believe that she wanted to make sure the next generation knew what had taken place. She must have realized they were witnessing history unfold. There were enough details for me to piece together the thread of their lives before I was even a speck of life meandering in the loins of my ma and my pa.

OUMAGROOTJIE

THE DAY KRISTINA descended on my farm it was like a dark cloud of screeching birds blanketed the blue sky. It foretold of the doom that was to befall us. It wasn't a happy chirping sound the birds were making, perhaps it was wailing. Maybe they were just plain angry, throwing a salvo of insults at the loskop khakis below them who were fighting for what they could have easily shared. All I know was that the birds were too disgusted to stay and be witness to all the foolishness.

The day the kaffir girl came down the mountain with her hands on her head she was squealing like a pig. She didn't even mind the dogs so you know things must be bad when a kaffir runs towards a farm dog without hesitation. Even the dogs seemed confused that day. Ears pricked, cocking their heads to the side, they were hesitant of their next move. Lately they had been cowering, the sound of gunshots and bombings taming them into pussycats.

The redneck tommies were burning everything in sight to smoke out the guerrillas. It was the scorched-earth policy by that cold-hearted Lord Kitchener. I had to remain calm but I had been expecting trouble to come to these parts. It had taken long enough.

"Annemarie, get her a glass of water," I commanded my bemused daughter. I kept my eye on the girl and Annemarie handed her a glass of water. The girl was hyperventilating and shaking like a leaf. "Aaklige goeters gesien. My eyes have seen a terrible sight, Madam. It is a terrible, terrible thing," she said, after gulping the water down in one go. Her name was Kristina Magubane and she had been pointed in my direction by a young kaffir who knew my Johan to be a good man.

She told me what she could still see in her mind—grim death and miles and miles of carcasses. An untold amount of livestock lying belly up, skinless, with bloated stomachs and their teeth exposed. They had been burned to death and the horrific smell of burning flesh hung thick in the air. It was almost as if the beasts had died having the last laugh at leaving the feuding fools behind. Black smoke shielded the sun, turning daylight into night. The sun was only too happy to have its eyes hidden from the atrocity. Evil doesn't like the presence of light; it thrives in darkness.

The misery of war begins when well-fed Boer women can feel their hip bones jutting out for the first time. When the smell between their thighs and their unwashed bodies stings their nose and when saliva collects in the corners of their mouths, watching as the lords eat the meat of the cattle stolen from their families' farms. When murderous thoughts dance in their heads as clean uitlander women offer to teach their children. It is when their skin is blackened by the sun until they begin to look like kaffirs themselves. It is when their children cry out in hunger until they die in their arms. It is when they bury their young on a daily basis and watch the once-respected godly elders slowly die from hunger and undignified dementia.

It is when randy, drunk soldiers come looking for tenderness in their hardened hearts. It is watching good church women succumb to performing sexual favors for a morsel of food for their children. It is when women can't look each other in the eye anymore because of what they have become. It is when theft and fist-fighting become the norm for women whose three cardinal purposes in life used to be their children, the kitchen and the church. Now they curse God, stealing, fighting and fucking for the bare necessities.

The grass was licked clean by the flames, countless walls of farmhouses standing like wounded soldiers—proud to be standing but bearing the scars of war. Blackened with soot, the thatched roofs were gone, burned to the ground. The screaming of captured Boer women and children was still a disembodied sound in the girl's ears as they were shoved into large cattle trucks to be sent away to the camps.

Those whose husbands were known and respected commandos in the guerrilla camps demanded special treatment. Even though the undesirables were already receiving much less than the first class. The first class cannot look the others in the eye out of shame for surrendering, and the undesirables pour scorn on them for being weaklings. Soon they feel it is only right to raid and steal what they can from the first-class tents. Death and disease spread like veld fire in the first three months in the concentration camps.

It is so quiet here on the farm that the girl eventually starts to wonder whether she really did see it all. Was some of it exaggerated in her head? Forget. That's what she wanted to do. She wanted to un-see what she had seen. Doubt was good, she welcomed it. She'd rather not be sure of what she saw than believe it. She didn't know how to relate to it all. And it wasn't the language that was being used that was the barrier; she had worked on farms and spoke perfect Afrikaans. Hell, her father was a Black Boer fighting in the war and now her lover had gone to join them. The thought of him hurt her and filled her heart with fear. She touched her belly—flat as a board—but she knew that she was expecting. The ignominy of the pregnancy reduced her to tears. She could never go home; she couldn't face her sister. She could not see her when she discovered that he had chosen her.

What that girl related to me that day was enough to convince me to launch into action. I dispatched twenty of Johan's birds to reach the farms on the unaffected side of the mountain. I knew those bloody tommies would die trying to get to each and every farm, including mine at some point. The message I sent with the birds had the biblical semblance of Noah's message in the Bible:

To those who want to continue the Boere way of life with no intention of giving in to the rooinek tommies, bring a heifer, a cock and a hen, one loyal female servant, seeds to plant and whatever little treasures you have. Ou Piet left us his bull to impregnate the

heifers. We will have milk, cheese and enough supplies to keep us
going until our men claim our land. Come in the cover of darkness,
be stealthy, the khakis are watching.

I didn't want to raise panic so I didn't mention anything about what the girl told me she had witnessed. I knew my neighbors well enough to know that some of them would not act if they heard it was in fact the kaffir girl who had seen the attacks. I also knew that some of them would not bring any servants since they would not have considered any of them to be loyal. Hell, some of the servants had joined the British, ratting out where the guerrillas were positioned. For what I couldn't tell you, perhaps the promise of mealies, mealie meal and beans, but I could just imagine some of the women ranting. The environment was incendiary and the madness of war plants the seeds of paranoia and suspicion.

The pettiness of it all was exhausting and my vision was bigger than worrying about mixing with the kaffirs. All I knew was that the more hands there were, the more ways there were of healing. The more mothers there were, the more mothering there would be to save the children and keep them out of the tommies' way.

More than ever, the older, loyal kaffir servants were needed for their knowledge of herbs to use for medicine, the right plants to delay hunger pains and ways of finding water not visible to an unknowing eye. I would have to learn to bite my tongue at times and to speak when necessary. What was all-important to me though was that the women of the surviving farms needed to stay together if we were to live to tell the tale.

≡

I was a painter and my Johan had been a sculptor. I had painted many kaffir women and girls over the years and they had always fascinated me, but I still hadn't captured that elusive quality about them. Was it a smile that played in the corners of their mouths or was it a mocking smile? Were they taunting me with that something unreadable behind their eyes? This illusiveness was more intriguing to me than the Mona Lisa. I had exhausted much of the painting material on the farm. Oh, the joy and surprise on the kaffirs' faces when they saw my finished work. It was worth every stroke of a paintbrush. Their faces broke like the morning sun with smiles, their eyes full of wonder. I knew that some of them thought I had some great power that could capture the image of a person just like a looking glass. It frightened some of them but others were as fascinated by their portraits as I was of their mystery.

For days I observed the kaffir girl and kept on sketching, chasing to capture that perfect portrait once and for all. I couldn't resist; the girl was a walking painting. Lost in her thoughts, she was unaware that I was doing a charcoal sketching of her. She was in traditional dress with strings of red and grey seeds snaking around her neck and the edges of her shoulders, halting near her pointed breasts and a strategically placed beaded cloth covering her womanly area. She wasn't a convert, I could tell by the way she was dressed. She was one of the last of the unconverted and was beginning to feel strange without clothing—a societal conformance. When I looked at the sketch, I couldn't believe what I saw. I was elated. In the middle of all the bloody war, I felt I had finally managed to capture the enigmatic essence of this girl.

The sketch was perfect and for a little while I forgot about the war, the hate, the defiance and the running. This was what sadness looked like, I declared to myself after gazing at the sketch. I promised myself that one day when the war was over, I would add color to the sketch and I would treasure it forever. I decided that wherever I went the sketch would go with me. The sketch showed big tears running down the girl's cheeks; her eyes had a faraway look in them of someone deep in thought. Her nose was flat and small above her pouting mouth, emphasized by the fullness of her lips. Her shoulders were strong and accentuated by the rope-like beads; her breasts were full and perky with darkened, pointy nipples. Her stomach was flat and beautifully curved on the sides. The sketch ended just above her navel.

I was never one for painting full bodies. The old country had enough of those. When I saw paintings done by explorers who painted naked, open-legged women with their pink center gaping like exotic fruit, I was revolted. The vulgarity of the images left me feeling scandalized. The slack-jawed, glassy-eyed men who pored over those paintings in a trance-like state left me weary. These kaffir girls had at least pushed me past my discomfort of painting breasts because they were in full view, compelling the painter to move past self-censorship, to move past the nurtured discomfort. But I would not go past that.

When it came to men, well, I could think of nothing more fascinating to paint. I always dreamt of painting *that* part of them but I would deny that all the way to my grave, of course. Something about those thoughts left me flushed and scandalized. All un-Christian kaffir men who still preferred scant loincloth were not allowed on the farm. I had told Johan that they made me feel uncomfortable and so he reluctantly commanded his servants to denounce their essence, to turn to the Lord and dress as good Christian men or leave his land. Some left disgusted, while others simply hung onto their essence but changed their clothes. What human being knows what is in the heart of men?

Johan was none the wiser whether real conversion happened for any of them or if it was simply that some of them changed their clothes to appease him. Some of the kaffirs were fascinated by clothes and some took to wearing them like it was second nature while others struggled. Some just wore the clothes to work and took them off as soon as they reached their compounds.

"How can we be free to work and dance in confining clothes such as these? That is why they cannot dance to save their lives," the kaffir men laughed among themselves.

Johan was reluctant to issue instructions on covering up, because truth be told, kaffirs captivated his artistic imagination too, especially the young ones, both female and male. Everything about the men with their strong, brown muscular legs glistening with sweat in the scorching sun, the sinew of muscle on their uncovered, perfectly rotund behinds captured his creativity. When they danced, sometimes Johan couldn't help himself and joined them, making a fool of himself with his two left feet. He had a practiced look of indifference, but trust me when I say he didn't miss a thing in his observations.

The nakedness of kaffirs distracted us both and of course we would tell you that it was all in the name of art. They were living art as far as we were concerned. Meanwhile the kaffirs blissfully lived their lives not knowing that by just being themselves, they affected the two of us in the ways they did. They were none the wiser because our thoughts were neither expressed nor acted upon. They were an unconfessed sin for Christians and unsaid supplications to the ancestors for the kaffirs for whatever musings they had of us.

Johan sculpted using wood and all his sculptures were of legs, strong legs, with every contour of every muscle sculpted to perfection and always ending just above the navel. I had put all of his sculptures away in the furthest corner of the bunker built under the farmhouse so that the women who were coming did not see them. What was art to some was deeply offensive to others. They would know that the sculptures were modeled by kaffir boys. There was only one way to tell but otherwise wood is wood and has no race. Nevertheless, I would not subject these women to the hysteria that I used to feel when I looked at the sculptures. After all, they were hot-blooded, mostly young women of childbearing age, and their men were at war.

Before Johan died, the kaffirs were confused and putting distance between them and Johan, which was puzzling to us. He displayed all the signs of a man with spirits but can a Boer really be with the spirits?

Silently and with knowing eyes, they kept their distance. They knew that without guidance, Johan would eventually jump into the dam he had built on the farm and commune with a large snake they believed sat at the bottom. Alas, this is exactly what he did. They all stood as far away from the water as they could when he was fished out, naked as the day he was born. I will never know what was plaguing my husband. We were compatible together and content with our work but perhaps the talk of war got to him more than he let on.

I did not wail like the kaffir women did; I held onto a tree, fell to my knees and growled like a wounded animal. The kaffir women stood in silence with tears conjured by sympathy. My daughter, Annemarie, who was about ten at the time, was confused and using the only comforting gesture she knew, stroked my back again and again, her big worried eyes looking on. The men stood, hats in hand, to mark the solemnity of the occasion. "He was a good, kind Boere baas," they murmured among themselves.

≡

The girl briefly told me how love had brought her to the Transvaal. "For my father and my lover, money brought them here. I know that everyone moves from one place to another because of something. I don't understand what makes the tommies do what they are doing?" She looked to me for an answer.

"It's the gold," I said and shrugged.

"Can you eat gold?" Annemarie asked.

"No, Antjie, but you can make a lot of money selling gold," I answered.

"The people who buy gold, what do they do with it?" the girl asked.

"Well, they make very expensive necklaces, earrings and other decorations for wealthy women in faraway countries."

"You mean to say that my lover is everyday putting himself in danger for a yellow metal that becomes a trinket and a decoration for women out there?" Kristina was clearly disgusted. Annemarie was thoughtful, imagining the kinds of women who wear these expensive trinkets.

"Do they know that people are being wiped out just so they can wear these trinkets?" the girl spat out the words without expecting an answer.

≡

The birds carrying my message reached the farms and altogether twenty women received my message after a week and some days. They mostly all know me and I would like to believe that they regard me with a mixture of respect and suspicion. Artists are known to be eccentric and, having run the farm alone for some time, if anyone was going to have a plan it was me. After some deliberation between themselves it became clear that they were better off together than alone. Some selected one of their servants to make the journey with them while others came only with their children.

The women made their way to Groot Dame, some over the mountain while others dared to cross the river on a wing and a prayer. Hoping that the crocodiles were full from eating all the animals, that must have felt like manna sent to them from heaven, trying to escape the fires started by the tommies.

I summoned the women to the table in the kitchen once they had all arrived. Kristina brewed coffee for thirty-odd adults, including the servants, and this was the first bone of contention for some of the women.

"Are we going to have to share everything with the kaffir servants?" Suzanne van Wyk asked, expressing what most of the women were thinking but not saying.

I asked her what she'd prefer we do, my voice thick with sarcasm and the resolution to bite my tongue quickly crumbling. And it wasn't even one day done yet.

"Well, couldn't we ration our supplies and have them deal with theirs in separate quarters to ours? We all know they have a different way of life to ours. That is what I do on my farm and it just makes things easier for everyone ..." her voice trailed off under the weight of all the eyes focused on her.

Some of the women agreed whole-heartedly while others made apologetic glances towards the silent kaffirs in their midst.

"Well Milly is looking after my twins so I cannot have them live in separate quarters to me," Rosie Grobler defiantly challenged Suzanne.

There was a long-standing grudge between the two women and the source of the tension was Kobus Grobler. He was Suzanne's childhood sweetheart before he met and married the spirited Rosie who, to add insult to injury, is of English descent, although she will have you know that she is in fact Irish and not English. As far as she's concerned, there is a big difference. Suzanne's bitterness over the rejection is still palpable. And little did we know then that one of Rosie's twins would grow and marry my Annemarie.

"Of course, who would expect the English to do their own dirty work? I have no doubt you were very happy to bring your own kaffir," Suzanne said, her voice escalating.

Milly looked down and muttered, "ikhafula unyoko msunu kanyoko," and a string of other isiZulu curses to Suzanne, who is known for her particular dislike of kaffirs. Suzanne threw her a stink eye but Milly said something about "an ugly face with cracked feet and fat ankles." I heard and understood it all but decided not to let on and struggled to keep my laughter silenced.

The other kaffir servants looked down but their shaking shoulders betrayed them. They were weak with laughter, prompted by Milly's string of skillfully put together insults all delivered with a straight face. Suzanne banged the table loudly with her hand.

"I will mos not put up with this. I would sommer rather go to the terrible camps than share space with this English woman conniving with the kaffirs who have no sense of loyalty!"

I squeezed my eyes in frustration, trying to bite my tongue.

Rosie snapped back at Suzanne, "I'll have you know that I'm Irish and married to a Boer. Do you think I like what is happening? Do you think you can hate the English more than me? I am as much of a Boer as you and so is Milly whose son and husband are side by side in the bush with your husband fighting those bloody tommies!"

Rosie's Irish temper was threatening to escalate the argument into a physical fight, her coffee mug ready to double as a dangerous weapon.

At one corner of the table, red-haired Onelia de Villiers began to cry softly and was soon full of gasps, her face and nose red with emotion.

"I'm so scared. We are all going to die without ever seeing our men again. Our land has been taken from us, our men are gone and now we are fighting with each other. Oh God, they are going to come for us." She carried on rambling until it became clear to everyone that Onelia had been self-medicating her fears with mampoer. She was as drunk as a skunk and I watched as a nightmare of misfiring feminine energy played itself out in front of me. I stood up and went over to Onelia and cradled her in my arms and let her cry it out.

"Dames," I said, "think of your children, think of your men in the trenches. We are all afraid and uncertain and it's human to lash out but ask yourself, how is it helping if we fight with each other? I asked for you to bring your servants because it is common sense that two hands are better than one and two brains are better than one. I'm glad to see Oude Milly is here and Margret and Nelisiwe because they know the soil and the water in ways that most of us don't."

The women listened in silence and I pointed to Kristina.

"You are here today because this girl had the presence of mind to come and warn me. I know that some of you had servants who did not think twice about joining the English and I do not have the answer as to why they chose that. But by the same token, the men of some of these servant women are fighting the war alongside our men. It is time we think of our children and for their sake get on with surviving this war the best way we can. Anyone who wishes to leave can do so but know that across the river the tommies are waiting. Your movements could put us all in danger. It would be a shame if a grudge held about things that happened many moons ago, over a man, nogal, puts all these lives in danger, including the lives of innocent children."

Suzanne folded her arms and sat down. She had two young children to think of and, although she wouldn't admit it, the thought of being alone terrified her. Onelia de Villiers sat drunkenly in the corner and snored softly throughout my pep talk but the message got through to the women and the matter was not discussed any further. Within a week, everyone gravitated towards those who they were comfortable with.

Groot Dame was a water- and mountain-locked farm with the river situated in the direction of the setting sun, the mountain, Klipriviersberg, in the east and the two man-made dams on the south and the north sides of the farm. It was ironic that the two things—the river and the mountain—that I initially hated the most about the farm and that made me feel so secluded and cut off, were proving to be the two things that saved us from the tommies, at least for a while. It was serendipitous that when Johan built the large farmhouse he created an elaborate bunker in the basement where he stored his sculptures. It was never with the thought of hiding from any war but it had come to that. But I wasn't under any illusion that we were completely safe. If Kristina knew how to find the farm, it was only a matter of time before the tommies suspected that there were Boers hiding here.

We all quickly settled into a daily rhythm, twenty women, ten servants and seven children ranging in age from a year old to my ten-year-old Annemarie. Rosie's twin boys, Liam and Cilliam, were the same age as her so she had plenty of company. Hostilities were still there and sometimes flared up but that was to be expected when there are so many anxious women living together.

Onelia was the supplier of the mampoer. Aside from the two chickens she had brought with her, she had laden her bags and that of her servant with nothing but moonshine. She seemed determined to drink herself into a stupor every day so that she did not have to think about anything else. Her fear and anxiety were palpable and infectious, especially in the mornings when she was sober. Her stash eventually dwindled, sending a few of the other women into a panic. I watched her closely because I suspected that I would have trouble on my hands once Onelia's "medicine" was finished.

Without her mampoer she went into withdrawal. She fiddled and fidgeted and constantly talked to herself. She went through all the empty containers of her moonshine, sticking her tongue into them, hoping for just one drop to wet her tongue. She refused to eat and scratched herself raw. Big, angry red welts appeared on her body and her behavior regressed to childish antics like bullying the children and swearing at the dogs. One day the servants found her in the bunker, naked as the day she was born, straddling one of Johan's sculptures that she had found. She was in the throes of ecstasy.

"Leave her be," Nelisiwe whispered to the other servant, Margret, who was mortified and ready to publicly rebuke Onelia's behavior. They backed way discreetly, leaving Onelia to please herself with the wooden sculpture. Nelisiwe consulted with me and I knew that if nothing was done, Onelia was going to be permanently lost to her fears and withdrawals. Her mind was leaving her. It was such a shame for a girl who was very religious and an all-round good person before this stupid war. Nelisiwe was affected the most by Onelia's sickness as Onelia and her family had always been kind to the servants.

"I have to help her. That girl's mother was the kindest church woman I ever knew," said Nelisiwe. She went foraging in the garden and came back with a triumphant smile on her face and a bunch of leaves in her hand. She began to grind the leaves, humming a tune to herself and to the plants. She then took a tin of water and brought it to the boil.

Nelisiwe said that if her plan to help Onelia came from me, the women would perhaps be willing to listen. I called the women together and asked for volunteers willing to help Onelia go through the treatment to cleanse her body of alcohol and calm her anxiety.

Curiosity filled their eyes.

"What do we have to do?" asked Suzanne, who had mellowed significantly since those early days on the farm.

"That tent over there has a bucket with a concoction

of boiling water and herbs in it. The steam from the water, mixed with the herbs, will help cleanse her. Five women can fit in there and sit with Onelia and keep her calm. It is good for the skin so you will have to strip naked for the medicine to work."

At the mention of sitting naked in a tent with a kaffir and a mad drunk, a few women backed off.

But surprisingly it was Suzanne, her arch-enemy, Rosie with her servant Milly, and Nelisiwe, who took the first shift in the tent. They held Onelia down through her torturous screaming. Some sang lullabies while others prayed for her throughout her screeching, which sounded like an exorcism of some kind was taking place. After a few days of the cleanse, Onelia started to sleep through the night without any episodes.

But Nelisiwe and I were not convinced that we were over the worst of it. Onelia's silence was not peaceful and it worried me because I had seen how she stared at the dam. It was disturbing. I noticed that she woke up earlier than anyone else and stood too close to the dam, watching the mist rise out of it like smoke. At times she had tears streaming down her face while at others she was silent and seemingly deep in thought.

I drew various portraits of ghostly Onelia standing by the misty dam; dark sketches soliciting melancholy from anyone who looked at them. Oddly, when I showed her the portraits they seemed to give her a new lease on life. She started to spend her days sketching and her demeanor changed. The shy, prayerful girl returned and her silence was no longer heavy and depressive.

≡

The women had taken to this new life better than I expected. We managed the farm with daily routines established, petty scores were settled and life waiting for the war to be over was lived.

It was the winter of 1901 and the women were watching a heifer in labor. Those who had given birth had an inkling of the pain, but it was pain that was soon forgotten after the first wailing of that new life. Forgetting is a universal illusionary lullaby, it seems.

"Come meisiekind, I want you to see this," I told Annemarie that morning. She was a tender-hearted, pretty little girl but there was no place for any princesses on the farm and so every opportunity to train her to be competent in survival was vital. It was early in the morning and the sky was glowing orange on the horizon. The heifer had been wailing for hours and the sound grated my ears until I could no longer stand it.

I called all the women, aside from Kristina who was sick and heavily pregnant by then and left to sleep, to come to the kitchen. Some of the women started the fire for the morning porridge and what was left of the coffee. There was excitement at the thought of buckets of milk, homemade cheese and rusks that Tannie Sunnelle's servant was going to make. It was exciting for Annemarie and as I watched her I was reminded of myself as a child.

The passing of time sometimes left me despairing and occasionally I wished I could join my beloved Johan. His death had finally become a memory that did not cause me great pain anymore but more of a longing. The war had forced me to become a survival expert and I felt responsible for all these women and children. I had to train the young ones and sharpen the girls into becoming steady women of stern constitutions who could stand with their spines straight. These men and their wars, senseless wars, one after the other, infuriated me.

The birthing of the calf that day was to be a rite of passage for Annemarie. The heifer was pacing back and forth and at times lying down. Her big eyes were full of fear as if she was asking, "What is happening to me?" The women, silent as stone, stood at a distance to give the heifer her space. It was like we were communing with her—united in the experience that binds women together. A strange ritual as if to say, "You are not alone, we are here until you are done."

Annemarie stood with us, feeling nervous, but trying hard to keep calm. I showed no sign of any action to be taken so we watched the heifer. The sun was now at the top of our heads and suddenly the heifer stood completely still. Its hind legs buckled and she let out a primal groan. We knew what the heifer was conveying.

After another groan, a wet sac emerged from the cow and hung down out of her birthing canal. It was a slimy, yellowish sac and I became concerned when I saw the calf's front legs were emerging first, pointing up to the heavens.

"Oh hel, daai kalf is breeching," Nelisiwe said quietly with controlled panic in her tone.

"Annemarie, here's your chance, meisiekind. You have

the strongest, most slender arms among us. I want you to keep calm and do as I say, you hear?"

Annemarie nodded and pushed up her long sleeves and the women greased her arm with lard. The heifer moved back and forth, the emerging sac partially withdrawing back inside the cow.

"We cannot afford to lose this heifer or the calf, Antjie. Meisiekind, steady yourself and put your hand in that birthing canal."

There was a murmur of panic among the women. "Pasop Annemarie, make sure she doesn't kick you!" the women warned.

Annemarie was a natural and made calming noises as she neared the back of the heifer. The poor thing was in so much pain and was utterly exhausted. Annemarie loved animals and she was willing to do anything to help the heifer. She gently entered the birth canal with her fist and in the warm gel-like fluid, opened her hand and tried to feel for the calf's muzzle still covered in the membrane. She navigated it out towards the opening of the birth canal and pulled out her arm and the calf fell out. The gel-like mess of birthing spewed out on the ground around the calf.

The women breathed a collective sigh of relief. Annemarie beamed with a sense of achievement and the women praised her steadiness. It was a miracle that the cow had survived at all with such meager feeding over the preceding months, with the earth bone dry and the flames that had licked everything in sight.

After the excitement of birthing the heifer, it was back to work and we all got on with our chores for the day. There was no time to be idle. Our men had gone and become guerrillas, the despicable khakis were taking over and forming colonies, and the two republics remained resistant with our vow as the occupants to fight to the death. Our deaths would not be on our knees; we would be standing with guns blazing.

The yellowish-green shoots of sweet kikuyu grass were sprouting, signalling fragile hope. The land was slowly recovering from the English assault. Mother Earth was once again rising up to feed her children, the same ones who torched her trees, her livestock and her many gifts. The women were steadied by the sparse greenery when they looked across the river separating them from the mayhem. The birthing of the new century had come with great pain.

$$\equiv$$

One night Kristina, who was weeks away from giving birth, was sitting around the fire with the other servants enthralling them with the story of how she got to the farm. Sometimes they burst out laughing, while at other times they clapped their hands. I was playing cards with the other women but I was listening carefully because she had never volunteered the entirety of it with me.

Kristina told the women it was the love of a man that got her to the farm. Mbongeni was meant to marry her older sister. His father wanted him to marry her because her sister was being educated at the mission school and having an educated makoti would bring more respect to his family. Mbongeni knew better than to argue but his eye was always on Kristina and she didn't mind that. In fact, she said it was most welcome. The women all giggled in unison. "Truth be told, he never liked the look of my older sister and told me about his predicament. He said that nothing about her was womanly."

He asked me what man wants to marry a girl who speaks her mind? Who looks him in the eye without smiling and being coy? Who defiantly goes to mission school to get an education when other girls stay at home? My sister unnerved him and he said that she was trouble on two legs. He felt bad for speaking ill of her but he was a simple man. He just wanted to make money on the mines and have a wife who would just be a wife, not a silent lioness in his house.

How do you begin to enjoy a future with someone when there is so much guilt to begin with? Kristina told the women that she loved and respected her sister but how was she to stop the river from flowing down the waterfall into the sea?

That's how it is with love. You don't choose, it happens. It strikes you down with a fever so hot the mind walks towards the north and the heart walks to the south, causing chaos and leaving behind ruins and betrayal. It is much like the war we are in now.

Kristina knew her sister well and she would let her guard down when they were alone, engaging in sisterly talk about boys. She secretly liked Mbongeni's adventurous spirit. He was one of the first in the village to move north to work on the farms and later on the mines. Adventure, excitement and new opportunities were things that brought a shine to her sister's eyes. She would talk of how when her and

Mbongeni got married she wanted to move to the city and teach in a proper school like the missionaries did. She had already made plans and Kristina just listened, filled with bitter jealousy. She couldn't imagine marrying anyone except Mbongeni. After stolen moments with him by the river, it felt like a little bird was kicking in her chest every time her sister spoke of her dreams, dreams made only on paper, of moving to the city, because Kristina knew she was going to be the one marrying Mbongeni.

Mbongeni thought of ways he could get out of marrying her sister, as his father dictated, and marry Kristina instead. They met at their secret meeting place by the river where she used to collect water and he told her his plan. He thought of me, the Matriarch as they call me, because he once worked here and knew I would help them. Kristina would come to the farm and he would go to the mines. If the war carried on he might join one of the fighting groups, as long as it was near the mine so he could continue working to save for lobola. Once the war was over, he would come back for her and they would return home. It didn't take much to convince Kristina and the promise of Johannesburg, gold and being with the man she loved was all she needed to hear.

So one cold morning they got a ride on a truck that was returning to the Transvaal after dumping a group of Boer women and children at a new camp in Howick. Kristina still shudders when she thinks of the scenes they saw on that drive. She started to worry that the farm would be burned to the ground by the time they reached it but Mbongeni said he was sure it would be standing if

I had anything to do with it. He was right and they had to part ways on the other side of the mountain to avoid leading the tommies to Groot Dame and she sprinted all the way here.

She wants to believe it will all be worth it in the end. That the war will be over and she will go home with her baby and a man ready to pay lobola to make it all go away. The shame of running away with a man intended for her sister will hopefully be forgotten, but she knows that will probably not happen. She hasn't had a telegram from Mbongeni since she got here and feels that when she alighted that truck that day it was the last time she would ever see him. They parted without him knowing he was going to be a father. She was a mess of tears and misery when she got here to warn me. The other servants comfort Kristina, encouraging her not to give up hope.

$$\equiv$$

With the birth of the calf happening only a few weeks prior, another birthing happens on the farm when Kristina goes into labor. As she stood watching Onelia pray next to the beautiful misty dam one morning, her water broke, the warm liquid sneaking down her legs. She looked down and then at old Nelisiwe, who was the leader among the servants and standing next to her.

"Look at me," Nelisiwe commanded Kristina, whose eyes were full of fear. "You are going to be fine. This will be over before you know it and your baby will be here. Do you feel any pain?" Kristina shook her head.

I spotted them from the veranda and I could see it was time for Kristina's child to come. I laid down the rugs and ordered someone to get warm water and lots of towels. Soon the farmhouse was a hive of activity. Nelisiwe walked slowly with Kristina to the kitchen and instructed her to kneel on all fours on the rugs on the floor.

"What is she doing? She should lie down on her back," said Suzanne van Wyk, but I hushed her. Nelisiwe was concentrating on Kristina and barking orders. The young ones, my Annemarie included, were shooed out of the house. Kristina was frightened into silence like the heifer had been at one point during her labor. She knelt on all fours and her heavy dress and apron were unbuttoned and taken off her, leaving her as naked as the day she was born.

The servants were in charge of this birth. Milly had collected dried-out grass and was burning it on a small plate and running the smoke under Kristina's nose while muttering supplications to the unseen higher beings. I was allowed to help and rubbed Kristina's back with a warm towel to try help ease her muscles. She started groaning as the contractions took over. Nelisiwe soaked her hands in salty water and then used two fingers to feel for the baby's head inside Kristina's birthing canal.

The Boer women had never seen this kind of birth and watched in silence as the servant women gave guidance and encouragement to Kristina. Nelisiwe instructed her to push; the head of the baby was crowning. She was stern in her commands and Kristina pushed with her knees and hands planted to the floor. Nelisiwe was in position as the baby's head popped out and after a few more pushes, the baby boy presented himself into her warm and salty hands. A whitish film covered his wrinkled body.

Nelisiwe inserted her finger into his mouth to clear out any mucous and he cried out, almost in disgust at being born into this warring world. He had good lungs on him and scrunched up his wrinkly face as he cried. Milly cut the umbilical cord and tied it in a knot. Kristina crumpled into a fetal position on the floor, exhausted and drenched with sweat.

Nelisiwe used a warm towel to rub the nipples of the new mother. She squeezed gently until a yellowish fluid began to leak out and helped the baby latch onto the nipple and suckle, which he did with gusto. All the mothers smiled and, even in her state of exhaustion, Kristina's eyes swept the room and she was grateful for all the mothers in her midst. Later, she fell into a deep sleep after naming the boy Kwazikonke Magubane. Onelia was so moved she began to cry while some of the other women swiftly wiped their own eyes, not wanting to be seen to be showing emotion.

Nelisiwe glowed with pride and talked to the baby as if he was hers. The women prepared porridge and tea for the nursing mother and mother and child were tended to with great care. The baby was loved by all the women, Boers and servants, and his birth solidified a bond among all the women. Grudges were forgotten and the focus was on survival, especially since supplies were thinning as the war dragged on.

We went through phases of hope and of losing hope and denial and fear and were clinging to each other, praying for each day to pass and a new one to begin. I improvised lessons for the children to learn the basics of sketching portraits, reading and writing their names. The women remained defiant despite what we knew was the inevitable advancement of the tommies. We refused to speak about it but we were all losing hope that the war was not abating.

We all hung on and stayed put, rationing what was left of our food and prioritizing the children. The heifer that had given birth was a godsend and provided us with ongoing sustenance. The grass and weeping willow trees grew back and hid us from any militia that may have been milling around. We had survived for more than a year until the winter of 1902 when our men finally returned home. I wish I could say we had won, but the British annexed our Transvaal and Orange Free State republics and called for an end to what they called "hostilities" but the Lord knows that the damage was done.

MADALA

ZOE AND I drink our hot chocolate in silence, both letting the words of my Oumagrootjie's diaries sink in. The diaries are yellowing but written in beautiful cursive. You could see Oumagrootjie had been an artist, even her handwriting was carefully crafted and neat. Her journals and the portrait of Kristina she had drawn were some of my most treasured possessions.

"Iyoo, Mkhulu, I'm learning so many new things from you. Either they hardly touched on this part of history at school or I wasn't listening."

"Ja, my Girlie, bloody 27,000 women and children didn't make it in those camps. Plus who knows how many soldiers lost their lives."

We are standing in the sunroom getting our mandated twenty minutes of sunshine. I can't bear to go outside because the winter breeze is too much for my papery skin.

We are a few months into this lockdown and Zoe has become much more than my night nurse. The rhythm of our stories flows from one day to the next and having her in lockdown with us at the home means we spend many, many hours together.

We are lucky that no one has contracted this sickness here in the home. A few of the old people went with their families before lockdown began but many wander around, confused by the lack of any visitors despite Ms. Rajah patiently explaining the lockdown.

"Do you know something, my Girlie, I sat with these diaries for years without reading them but I always knew there was something important in them. I only started to read them when I took out my pension before they called me back to the academy as an adviser. Those three months with no routine were nearly the undoing of me so they came in handy to help abate my boredom and the sense of uselessness that was eating me alive."

We walk back to my room and Zoe waters the potted plants on the windowsill, nipping off the dying leaves. She offers to make me a cup of coffee and makes a pot of tea for herself. She is enthralled by my Oumagrootjie's stories and wants to hear more. She says I remind her of Gogo Tu when I talk about Kristina and that she loves her without ever meeting her. I also think the storyteller in her has been piqued. I go on and tell Zoe the story about the next stage of my Oumagrootjie's life.

=

It turns out that Rosie Grobler, one of the women who took refuge at the farm during the war, was my other Oumagrootjie who married my great-grandfather, Kobus Grobler. He came back from the war and was a stranger to her, with unnerving silences pregnant with things untold. He left for the war a different man; a man who had a list of never-ending jokes and the skittishness of youth. He was barely a man when he left but he was already a skirt magnet, tempting even the staunchest Christian daughters to steal away with him to the riverbanks for stolen kisses. Then Rosie came along and made an honest man of him and gave him twin sons, Liam and Cilliam. She amassed many girl rivalries in the process. It seemed puzzling how the son of a Boer could end up with a foreigner of Irish descent, but pain attracts pain and, invisible to the naked eye, they both carried their own.

But the hope of a happy marriage didn't last for Rosie. War had taken the Kobus she had fallen in love with and had brought back a nightmare. Untold horrors drained the spirit out of him and alcohol loosened his tongue, but they weren't words of love that came out. His insults and abuse were despicable affronts layered with ignorance and hate and Rosie became his punching bag. He took his hatred for the British out on her despite the fact that the Irish hated the British too.

His eyes had seen war and its cruelties and what the British soldiers had done to the Boer women and children and he couldn't reconcile that he had married a woman so closely linked to the British.

Their twin boys, Liam and Cilliam, grew up around

their father's alcoholism and his anger and bitterness. Liam drifted off to the mines in search of gold as soon as he was old enough to leave, putting as much distance between him and his family as possible. And to get away from the constant arguing with his brother over a girl, Annemarie. Cilliam's romance with Annemarie flourished without his brother around. He had become a thorn in his brother's side and they had always competed over Annemarie, who couldn't seem to make up her mind who she wanted to be with. They had been like brothers to her growing up during the war but once puberty arrived a complex set of rules kicked in.

Liam made it easy by disappearing to the mines so Annemarie chose Cilliam. Their romance culminated in a pregnancy that was quickly covered up by a marriage before she started showing. Oumagrootjie and Kristina hustled up a feast and all the women who had stayed on the farm, including the servants, came together for what became a reunion as well as a celebration of young love. Kristina said it was a balm for everything they had put up with during the war. Everyone always knew that Annemarie would end up with one of the Grobler twins and so the conspicuous absence of Liam at the wedding was not a surprise. They had all helped raise the children during the difficult years of the war so the wedding was a celebration of many things. Annemarie was glowing and only Oumagrootjie, Kristina and Rosie knew that by the end of that year there would be a little Grobler greeting the world.

=

My ma, Anneke, was born into a new South Africa called the Union of South Africa. Her arrival calmed the rift between Rosie and Kobus, who became doting grandparents, and Liam and Cilliam renewed their brotherly bond. Liam met a girl on the mines and became one of the young Randlords, having made connections that led him to the money. My ma was a "Born Free" of the time since the British were finally withdrawing and leaving the country in the hands of the Afrikaners. Something sinister was brewing for the Blacks who continued to pay the price of war and greed. They were not included in any negotiations and the promises made to them by the British came to nothing. The new Boer government was ready to inflict maximum punishment on them for the betrayal of fighting with the English. The memory of the camps was still fresh in the minds of the Boers and so they began to chip away at the basic human rights of the natives.

"That is how the system concretized itself as the home of the mess we are in today, my Girlie. My mother was born in the throes of it all and I came into it once it was rule of law."

$$\equiv$$

Abject poverty after the war pushed Cilliam and Annemarie to join Liam in the Cape. He was dealing in exports using his neutral name to work with foreigners and had become very wealthy. Cilliam and Annemarie had been in the Cape for a few years when the Spanish flu hit, adding more misery to a country that was battling to recover from war. It hit young adults the most, with the return of soldiers from World War I carrying it in their lungs. Annemarie tended to both Liam and Cilliam, who both eventually succumbed to the flu. Alone, with a young child and frightened witless, she needed to get back to the Transvaal. She climbed on a train filled with Jewish orphans who were destined for orphanages in Johannesburg. She sent a telegram to Oumagrootjie saying she didn't know if she was going to make it home as she suspected she had contracted the flu herself while tending to the brothers.

By the time she got to Johannesburg, Annemarie was showing the early signs of the flu. When she arrived, Oumagrootjie, who had traveled alone from Groot Dame and left Kristina behind, let out a sigh of relief. The death of Kristina's son and her beloved Mbongeni had broken Kristina and she swore she would never go back home and face her shame. At that time, the mixing of Blacks and whites in trains was outlawed, causing huge protestations from Black leadership structures. Blacks were given limited space on the trains so Kristina was resolute that she would not be treated as a second-class citizen and stayed at the farm. She told Oumagrootjie to make the journey alone and to bring back her daughter and granddaughter. Annemarie made it home but soon lost the battle against the flu. Kristina later said that something changed in Oumagrootjie after Annemarie's death.

There was a sense of numbness in the country. Kristina had lost her boy and Rosie and Kobus were both gone too. Anneke survived and was raised by both Kristina and Oumagrootjie. She took to drawing portraits just like Oumagrootjie and together their art went a long way to save them from starvation. Curators from far-flung countries came to buy their work, but Oumagrootjie would turn them away and only dealt with a lovable young Dutch collector who had known Cilliam during his time in the colony. She remained loyal to him and felt a connection to him. Kristina called the man "Gimpy" because he had a limp.

Kristina once said that Gimpy had a tense stand-off with Oumagrootjie over a picture hanging on the wall in the living room. It was a beautiful drawing from Johan of a famous painting of a scowling, naked woman climbing out of a bathtub. Gimpy desperately wanted the piece but Oumagrootjie refused and said, "Nooit nie, never, I'm saving it." The women laughed, remembering Gimpy and his insistence at wanting to buy the picture.

Gimpy then told Oumagrootjie and Kristina the story of the original 1896 painting by a French artist called Jean-Léon Gérôme titled *Truth coming from the well armed with her whip to chastise mankind*. He told them that the story behind the painting was meant as a cautionary tale. Kristina said she would remember the story until the day they buried her six feet under.

Gimpy went on to tell them the story. Truth and Lies were making small talk but Truth was distrustful of Lies. When he said it was a nice day, Truth looked up to the sky to confirm it for herself. When Lies dipped his hand in the well and said the water was nice enough to swim, Truth checked the water herself to confirm. She confirmed that the water was indeed nice to swim in and stripped off her clothes and jumped into the well with Lies. But just as she was settling in the water and frolicking with Lies, he climbed out of the water and took her clothes. He put them on and walked around as if he was Truth. Truth climbed out the water, fuming that Lies had made a fool of her and she ran after him demanding her clothes back. The people shamed her for walking around naked and no one was interested in her explanation. The people preferred Lies dressed as Truth. They didn't want to see the real naked Truth and so naked Truth climbed back in the water and sank into its depths.

Oumagrootjie said that after hearing that story the picture had more value than any money that Gimpy would have given her. So Gimpy backed off and bought all of Johan's sculptures and paid Oumagrootjie enough money that she would never know poverty again. This meant that Oumagrootjie and my ma were free to paint together purely for the love of it and not to make money. My ma discovered a love for drawing wildlife and vast landscapes. She was well into her mid-20s when she finally met a man she felt was suitable for her, Adriaan van Rooyen, my pa. He was a photographer of wildlife so the two bonded over their shared passion. He soon asked for Anneke's hand in marriage and Oumagrootjie was so happy that her granddaughter, who had been in danger of being a spinster for waiting so long to walk down the aisle, was going to be a wife. Oumagrootjie was already steadily surrendering to old age but the union gave her a new burst of wilful living.

=

Years passed after my mother's death and I must have been about seven when Pa finally came back from fighting in the war. He looked important and stern and there were no hugs and kisses from him; in fact, it felt like he sucked out all the oxygen at the farm. Kristina and Oumagrootjie seemed so small and shrunken when he stood next to them demanding to know why Oumagrootjie was breaking the law by allowing a kaffir to live in the farmhouse and not in the compound like the other kaffirs. He had a snarl on his face that made me hang onto Kristina's pinafore. It felt like his eyes were boring into me and he said he was back to teach me how to be a "proper" Van Rooyen man. I tell you, indoctrination is a hell of a thing. I don't know if it was in those trenches fighting the war or the poison that was all around us but my pa wasn't anything I had expected him to be. He was nothing like the man that Kristina had told me about. I felt a mixture of awe and fear.

Kristina clapped her hands. "They got to you too, didn't they? Well, Big Master, I will take what's mine and move back to the compound. I don't want no trouble with the Groot Baas."

Oumagrootjie was straining to say something but no words were coming out and I was whimpering as Kristina was packing her belongings.

"Boy! Sit down and stop hanging onto the apron of that old woman!" instructed my pa.

He thundered so loudly that I almost jumped with shock. His voice took my breath away, my ears were ringing and my heart was thumping. I stood and watched and little did I know that that moment was the beginning of my miseducation. Kristina left for the compound, despite Oumagrootjie's appeals to my pa. A young nurse was hired to look after Oumagrootjie and the farm was run like an army from then on.

The workers seemed afraid and Pa worked them from the crack of dawn to sundown, fixing the buildings on the farm, weeding, dipping stock and tending to everything else that he thought was wrong and needed fixing. He had long talks with me about the importance of being a different breed to the kaffirs and demanded that the workers all address me as "Klein Baas," Young Boss, and respect me as someone who was going to run the farm and be their baas in the future. Kristina stood at a distance, her arms akimbo, shaking her head.

The day I stopped sneaking off to visit Kristina at the compound was after he caught me sitting with her and eating her homemade toffee. He marched towards me and yanked me off the chair I was sitting on. I started wailing and Kristina's voice was so stern that even he seemed confused. "Adriaan van Rooyen," was all she said. Her old face was so enraged and she would have hit him if she could. "Stop punishing this child for the things he doesn't know anything about, do you hear me? I'm telling you, otherwise you will never find peace."

He still had me in his grasp, his face snarling at Kristina. I think he was about to slap her but an unmistakeable growl from Jock, the pitbull that followed Kristina and never moved back to the farmhouse, stopped us all in our tracks. With a growl so fearsome, he was ready to sink his teeth into Pa. "Pasop, jou, watch out. I never want to see you here again and if you so much as lay a finger on that boy, you will know the wrath of the dead." Kristina spat on the floor in front of him. She shouted after him as I was frogmarched home. He didn't touch me or say a word to me that whole evening.

When I turned ten, Pa said I was a man and I needed to fend for myself so he shipped me off to boarding school in Natal. Oumagrootjie handed me a big, heavy box the day I left and put a note written in her neat but shaky handwriting, in my hand:

> My laatlammetjie, you are a good boy. The things in this box are my heart and I want you to have them. By the time you read them, I will be long dead but I will be sitting on your shoulder watching you learn. Be courageous and always maak 'n plan like your Oumagrootjie.

My first act of courage was to look Pa in the eye the day I left for Natal and request that I go and say my farewell to Kristina at the compound. I was shaking so much that I think he felt sorry for me. He agreed and I shot out the door before he could change his mind. I was running so fast that I nearly knocked Kristina off her feet with my forceful embrace and held her tight for a few minutes. She shoved a small bag of still warm toffee into my pants to hide it from Pa and leaned on her stick and looked at me.

"We survived the wars and we survived that flu that killed so many, what more could we ask for? I know you will find your way out there. Go well my child and always remember the story of the naked Truth. She is right here," and she poked my chest and kissed my forehead.

Walking back to the house, I stopped next to the tall mealies and waited for my tears to stop. I got back, quickly splashed my face with cold water and hoped the feeling like a stone that was lodged in my throat would pass. Pa didn't even drive me to school; he dropped me off with the Van Vuuren boys and we were driven there by their parents.

I didn't really understand what was happening, but looking back I realize my pa didn't want to be reminded of the wife he had lost and I reminded him of her every time he looked at me. I was already a damaged child, who desperately wanted to impress him, but I also hated him with everything I had. Boarding school cemented the indoctrination he had started and I wanted to belong and fit in so badly that I took dares, I picked fights, I made racist jokes and bent over backwards to be one of the boys. Once I hit puberty, I couldn't stand looking at the compound and seeing Kristina watching me when I went home during the school vacations. At first I would look and wave but the first time she worked out that I was ignoring her, she laughed a laugh that pierced right through me.

"Ah they got to you too, huh? Hamba juba bayok'chutha phambili. Fly little bird; they will pluck your feathers ahead. Always remember the naked Truth. She's going to climb out of the water any time now."

I never saw Kristina again after that.

The boys at school loved my antics, even the taunting and bullying of other boys and they called me fearless "Malkop." I was muscular like Pa but I still never felt enough.

Oumagrootjie died a few years later and Kristina followed a week after. I was stunned when I heard that

Pa allowed Kristina to be buried on the farm right next to Oumagrootjie. I attended Oumagrootjie's funeral but I wasn't requested for Kristina's and only found out about it the next time I went home. The only thing that consoled me was that they would be right next to each other for all eternity.

$$=$$

I stop, feeling too drained to carry on. I tell my Girlie to leave me for the night so she tucks me in and leaves. I toss and turn thinking about Kristina and it feels like my bed is whirling around and only in the early hours of the morning does sleep finally come. I wake with the winter sun shining on my face. I'm already in the sunroom when Zoe comes in with two mugs of hot chocolate. There is no sign of any strain on her face. I asked her to leave the night before because I was reaching parts of my story that I hate about myself. I feel like I'm wading through a pool of sewage.

Ou Stephan has been taken to isolation because he tested positive for this virus. Zoe assures me that everything is under control and that the whole place will be sanitized from top to bottom. I am looking at my Girlie closely for any signs of shock about what I told her the night before but it isn't an act, she really isn't judging me for what I told her about Kristina.

I want to ask her why when we hear a commotion coming from the TV inside. The news is on and it shows a Black man lying on his stomach with a policeman holding his knee on the back of the Black man's neck. The crowd is screaming at the policeman and I recognize the tension on his face. It makes me think of a pitbull locking its jaws on its target. We watch dumbfounded and Zoe goes online and confirms it is not a hoax. I feel unwell and she guides me to sit down. We both leave our hot chocolate untouched, reeling as we watch history unfold. After a few more minutes, she switches off the TV. "It's too much to take in, Mkhulu, sometimes it's best to give it a break."

We spend most of the day lost in our own thoughts, not saying much and feeling like the earth is spinning at full speed. In the days to come, we watch the TV as years of unspoken anger spill onto the streets. People everywhere are braving this virus to go outside and make it known that systemic racism has to end, that police brutality is enough. We watch a protest on the streets of Bristol in England and see the crowd pull a statue into the river, eliciting roars from the crowd as it splashes into the water.

Something shifts inside me. I think it's the whiteness of the boy who climbed the statue and the symbolism of it makes me realize that this is what I want for my unknown grandchildren. I want a different future for them and I want none of my family curses imbedded in their genes; there must be no shadow following them.

I turn to Zoe, "Remember what you said the other day, my Girlie? That underneath the veneer of our manicured lawn is a soup of maggots and dormant lava of hot red pain? You said your fear was that the day it was activated it would wipe us all clean. Well, it's happening."

She looks at me with such sadness in her eyes.

"It's going to take some time, Mkhulu. It's going to take some heavy lifting to change things. Nothing is more resolute than the system that's running us right now. It's difficult because everyone thinks they are doing the right thing," she says thoughtfully.

I don't really understand what she is saying but I don't ask her to explain. I'm trying to figure this all out for myself. I keep hearing that Black people are tired of explaining things to us.

"Us whites have been so blind to your experiences as Black people and its only now that we are learning to walk. For most of my adult life I believed that there was something inherently childlike about Black people. And now, in a matter of days, I feel completely exposed as the ignoramus with no tools to navigate this world that wants equality. White people are experts on how to live in an unequal society, ignoring anything that threatens to shift our view. When apartheid officially ended most of us said we didn't know it was that bad. The English became bleeding liberals who grasped at any small gesture or change to claim they fought for liberation. Nothing is hidden anymore; we are watching this all in real time."

I can see Zoe is processing what I've said as I still try to work out what she meant by her statement.

"It's like this, Mkhulu. Do you remember the Boipatong massacre in the nineties and the exposé of the so-called third hand? We used to call it the hairy hand and the third force. Now look at the protest slogans like 'I can't breathe.' Does that make you feel hopeful? And look at the symbol used for 'kneeling on the floor' after the horrific way that policeman killed that man. What does that tell you? These slogans of not breathing and kneeling are casting powerful spells. Spells that are pronounced constantly and on a daily basis continue to grow and automate. We are already not breathing and our emotions are ahead of our minds. Anyway, it's a long story, Mkhulu, but what I can tell you is that they can keep kicking a dying horse but it will not go down without a helluva fight. We just need to hang on. We'll soon hear about the third force and it is a force far bigger and stronger than the uncouth nationalists in the nineties."

$$\equiv$$

I still don't get what Zoe is trying to say but what do I care? I'll be gone before all the shit really hits the fan. The idea of death emboldens me to tell her everything and have my own one-on-one TRC hearing. She has become so important to me that I know I will regret it if I die without telling her what I did. Part of her pain, of losing her mother like she did, is linked to what I once believed was my mission to save my country from communists. Belief is a hell of a thing and now I know what Kristina meant when she said they got to me too.

"Ja, nee, my Girlie, brainwashing takes many forms. Look at what it did to me. In 1957, the year I turned eighteen, the year the SADF had its first intake. I committed all sorts of despicable acts with impunity while I was in the army and I was proud of that. Predestined shame is a patient thing. It will stalk you quietly and not show up when you think it will, but it will nevertheless show up right on time. It is like an untrained mutt that digs up soiled diapers and bloodied sanitary pads and kills the neighbors' chickens."

≡

At first we spent most of the time training and performing dry runs. Although there was tense talk of independence in our neighboring countries, Namibia, Angola, Zimbabwe and Mozambique, it was only much later that we went into combat with guerrillas trained in the Eastern bloc and Cuba. We all knew and smelled fear. The guerrillas were relentless on the borders and gave us hell and in the process we became hardened beyond repair. Those men and women knew every inch of the soil they were stepping on and would creep up on us and have us surrounded in minutes. We had to learn to use all our senses to stay alive. Young boys were required to serve a minimum of nine months and we did not take kindly to any "bangbroek" excuse to dodge conscription. We physically and metaphorically crippled a nation of people and debased so many boys during those fourteen years on the border. Making sure that we hindered the independence of people who were the rightful custodians of the land.

I come from rotten, rancid and putrefying hollow roots. No one went there. Instead, it was ignored, covered up and decorated and left alone, hoping it would right itself. Around me there were manicured lawns, high-walled houses, deep blue swimming pools, two dogs, a maid to keep the house shiny and a garden boy to keep the garden tidy. But the pervading and odious smell of manure stayed with me, a reminder of the rot lurking just below the surface of all this perfection. Can anyone really reverse decades and decades of this? I didn't think so. In those days I was well conditioned to un-see it all. But I couldn't un-feel it or un-dream it. The human body keeps score; there is not a single incident it doesn't store somewhere to use later on.

≡

I met my wife, Sidney Johnson, in 1964 while I was at the coast on a break from the army. I was laying low for a while with all the buzz that was happening with the Rivonia Trial. She reminded me of a frightened springbok, beautiful but very skittish and nervous. I was so messed up, I was just basically looking for a girl who would give me children and never talk back or have any ideas of her own, so she seemed perfect. I never saw my father love anyone when I was growing up. The woman he eventually ended up with endured his abuse and I couldn't bring myself to go home anymore during my breaks. She was jumpy and frightened at the sound of his voice and I would leave with a naar feeling in my stomach after those visits. Plus, the farm was no longer my home after Kristina and Oumagrootjie died. The farm itself was thriving and running better than it ever had, but it was like it had also died. It was ghostly cold and there was no warmth in the hearth.

Our wedding was attended by all my boys from the army and Sidney's family from Durban. I was in my full army regalia and I think I had a rare moment in my life of being happy. I was going according to the script of what it meant to be a good Boereman and marrying a God-fearing woman to bear my children. I deviated slightly by taking on an English woman. She was like a bird that lightened my load and I did love her, but in a messed-up sort of way. I fed off the feeling of terrifying her just like my father did. Sidney never knew what would set me off and I got worse after the Border Wars. Seeing so much inhumane killing left me teetering on the edge of insanity. Sidney gave birth to my boy in 1969 and I was filled with a mixture of terror and pride. I was hoping we would have a boy as there was nothing I could have done with a girl. I had seen what happened to girls who joined the guerrilla wars. In our psychotic and crazed states, we raped those girls and threw their bodies in the veld for the vultures and God knows whatever else. Taking a life became a non-issue, but their defiance and cries were like tons of bricks weighing on my psyche.

Things only got worse between 1975 and 1980, with the liberation movements relentless in their fight for the sovereignty of their countries. Me and my men had to deliver news to families that their sons were not coming home. Those were the saddest times. Young boys left home excited and proud and came home crazed, blathering things in their sleep, the pop of a balloon having them diving for cover. Many a harmless birthday celebration was ruined. Parents' crestfallen faces bemused by post-traumatic stress eating up their sons.

My poor son bore the brunt of my unstable mood swings. My presence in the home sucked out any joy and my son, like my wife, was afraid of me. Laughing one moment, the next I would lash out at either him or his mother. Sidney changed too and sometimes I think she hated me. On many occasions I had my way with her, even when she was openly objecting. I was violent with her and didn't know how to be tender. I was thrusting at things that were chasing me in my head. Sometimes the demons were so bad I would break down and cry and only the four walls of my bedroom witnessed my moments of weakness.

Talk of releasing Mandela sent shock waves through the country. For some years the country had started experiencing "brain drain" or "white flight" where white people uprooted their lives to get away from the Blacks ruling the country. In the force, we began to bury many of our men who committed suicide. I had left the army by then and joined the police force, dealing with MK's sabotage attacks. The fact that nothing was ever pinned on me all those years later during the reconciliation was because of a balaclava; I used it consistently to cover myself in our filthy missions.

In 1987 my son was sent to serve his conscription. It was tense in our home and Sidney was beside herself with worry. I was too because the year opened with an attack on soldiers in Alexandra township. Knowing everything that I knew, there was no way I could prepare him for what he was going to face. I was plagued by terrible nightmares and it was the year that Sidney shocked me into leaving her. Her rejection of my advances were fierce and we would fight until I overpowered her.

One day she lay very quietly until she knew I was at my weakest and then she attacked. I had had too much to drink so she gripped my midriff and, with her legs, she squeezed my chest. Gasping for breath, I was in a state of shock. I knew that move, it was an unmistakeable tactic used by guerrilla women who killed many a randy soldier. But unlike Sidney, they aimed for the neck. Quicker than a mamba strike, they would grip a man between their solid thighs and twist. Men would be found with their pants down and their necks broken.

I struggled for breath, my eyes bulging. That's when I realized why my team was always one step behind our targets. Sidney and our maid, Sophie, were infiltrating our information and alerting UDF structures of our plans. I was sleeping with a snake.

Sidney's voice sounded like a stranger's. "Now listen to me you bloody fucking bastard. This is the last time you force yourself on me. Touch me without my permission and I swear I will end you even if it kills me."

She squeezed a little harder and then pushed me off. She went into the bathroom to have one of her long showers to scrub me off her. I was sober by that point and knew that if I didn't leave, I would eventually kill her. I had been thinking of transferring from Durban to Pretoria anyway to get away from anything that would point to me when they finally began their witch hunt. Some of our men were so spooked we knew they would sing like canaries if put under any pressure.

I couldn't look at Sidney; she had shaken me to my core and I was filled with such shame. By that stage, my son wasn't talking to me and we'd had so many rows over my abuse. At eighteen years old, he was tall and strong and he knew he could stand his own against me if it came to that. We were two bulls in one kraal and I'm sure he was relieved to see the back of me, even if it meant he might die in his infantry.

≡

I must have dozed off at this point because I suddenly jerk awake. My face is wet and Zoe has two fingers at my throat checking to see if I am still breathing. When I open my eyes, she lets out a sigh of relief. I try to say something but she hushes me, shaking her head and reminding me of Billie Holiday's "Hush Now Don't Explain."

"Sleep Mkhulu, you've exerted yourself. We'll pick this up again tomorrow."

I can't tell what she is thinking but I'm too tired to even think. I feel the days counting me down to meet the Grim Reaper and I'm ready. I can go knowing that at least one person, especially this person, knows all of me and my shame. I drift back to sleep.

≡

Unbeknownst to me, after I tell her the story about my family, Zoe starts scouring the internet looking for my son. She finds a series of articles written by a blogger called Joseph Johnson-Van Rooyen and there is a picture byline that accompanies the articles. She has no doubt it is him because the resemblance between us is uncanny. He mentions his mother, Sidney Johnson, and Zoe knows it is a race against time to try to find the person behind the article, to give him the opportunity to say his piece and say goodbye to a dying man.

—

I wake up the next day and Zoe is snoring on the couch with her laptop on her chest. I let her be and go into the sunroom. The winter sun seems to brighten everything outside despite the dry brown grass and bare trees. There is a green aloe flourishing in the sunroom. Its self-reliance and lack of need for constant watering makes me feel free and a little bit stronger than yesterday. I have released something and it didn't kill me.

When Zoe wakes up, we have our hot chocolate in silence. I go back to my Oumagrootjie's box of journals and Kristina's portrait and hand them to her.

"I want you to have these, my Girlie. Keep them, throw them away or sell them. Do what you want with them, but they are yours. I could never repay you for what you have done for me. You have listened to things that I never thought I would ever tell another living soul and yet you are still here."

She takes them from me with tears in her eyes. We look at each other, unable to hug during these times. We are free-falling towards the end of June and the end of her contract, but what Zoe hasn't told me is that she has extended her time here until the end of the year. From then on, we put the stories aside and are still. She is on her computer while I read the newspaper and doze on and off. Whatever she's reading must be good because she's lost to the world for hours on end, only looking up to take meals and drink hot chocolate in between harmless chit-chat.

I later find out that she was reading about the other piece of the puzzle of my life, my son, Joseph. Who was ridding himself of his demons by putting pen to paper about his early life with me as his father. And it seems that I wasn't far off from what *my* father had been to me—a horror.

JOSEPH

BABIES STARE WHEN they suckle or when their head is cradled in the crook of an arm. I had many opportunities as a baby to read Sophie. Even as a small child I knew things about her, like her moods and sometimes her restraint. I knew when she wasn't paying attention to me and I would fuss. I knew when she was sad because she cried openly, her warm tears dripping onto my chubby face. As a small boy I remember gently touching her face with my stubby fingers, hoping she would be comforted by my gesture. She would wipe her tears and swaddle me tightly with a towel on her warm back and go about her day. I was on her back so much that my one knee, still today, bends out slightly crooked resulting in a slightly bowed leg, typical of many Black children who spent hours on their mother's back. It was a source of great shame for my father but it gave me a slight edge later on when girls started to notice me.

There were magic times when Sophie would match my intent stares with pure love like I was her baby. I'd giggle and she'd match my giggle with laughter that sounded like water bubbling from a brook. For a while it felt like the world was pure and perfect. Before you ask me how I could possibly know all of this back when I was in diapers, I firmly believe that behind the intent gaze of a baby, they know things, they see things, they think things. Indulge me and my theory for a bit, will you?

Blood is blood and I am my father's son but when I turned seven, I was more Sophie's than I was my parents, Hans van Rooyen and Sidney Johnson. My ma was so dominated and mentally beaten down by my pa that she was barely there to be a ma. Sophie taught me to take things with both hands and to say thank you. When I said "Ma" for the first time, it was to Sophie not my mother. We hid a lot of things in our family so that was ignored, but I think I knew that I was rejecting my lot, that I already wanted out of there. I felt the hollowness, the secrets and the confusion and, most of all, fear that was so rank you could smell it. As a grown man I cry inwardly when I glance at any elderly Black woman who reminds me of Sophie. I never knew where she ended up.

I knew just by her look when I had to stop my nonsense. I knew by the tone of her voice and when she called me by my full name, Joseph Johnson-Van Rooyen. But she never did it when my father was around. When he was, Sophie was not bossy with me; she was strained, guarded and unsettled. My world felt like a dark song being sung underwater and, like Sophie, I played along to survive. I had a false self for my father and was my true self when I was with Sophie. Later, I became a convoluted mess and didn't know which self was true and which was false. Sophie taught me respect and she also taught me when to show my true self to others and when to protect myself. Looking back, this shape-shifting of my character became something I used to get by in life.

In 1979 I was ten years old and I was having nightmares almost every night. I was scared of my father and so I tried very hard not to disturb him or my mother. I could never relax around him, no one could. Some days he would be calm and loving and other days he'd be violent and vicious. He was quick with his swift, sharp backhand either to me or my mother. It was like a reflex and, at the slightest provocation, his strike could send us flying backwards, heart-stopping heat on the flesh where his hand had connected. His presence in our house felt like it sucked out all the oxygen and heat, leaving us breathless and cold.

Sophie found me every morning drenched in sweat, my pyjamas and sheets soaked through. Sophie and I had an understanding and we kept it a secret. We communicated wordlessly those dark mornings, her wise eyes full of compassion and mine pleading with her not to tell my parents. The thought of my father finding out, frightened me witless. I used to think Sophie was also scared of him but she wasn't frightened, she loathed him.

Ironically, she was my refuge in my waking hours but in my dreams she tortured me. I'd dream that I was alone at home and she would let herself in the house and wouldn't be wearing her maid's uniform. She had tight camouflage overalls on with a black beret and a machete in her hand. Her face was full of all-consuming rage. She would point at me with the machete and march me to the bathroom. There she'd shove me towards the bathtub and order me to get in the empty bath and lie down. I'd plead with her with my eyes. My voice was gone, my mouth was bone dry and my throat constricted. I couldn't scream, I couldn't move, I was at Sophie's mercy. My fear fed her; it spurred her on and it satiated her. Then she'd open the cold water tap full blast until the water covered me and I started drowning. It would always be at this point in the dream that I would wake up.

This nightmare was so persistent that it eventually became so familiar and I would calm myself down knowing that if I waited long enough, my limbs would loosen and I would shake myself back to life. I didn't feel in any danger when I was with Sophie. I had learned to separate the Sophie who covered for me and the Sophie who drowned me every night.

≡

The lines between "madam" and "maid" were sometimes blurred between my mother and Sophie. They talked like friends, they cried and laughed together, but things were a certain way back then. For them, being who they were was generational. Sophie's mother took over from her mother who was working as a maid for the Johnsons and so it was only natural that Sophie followed. That she took over the trade of cleaning houses, raising other people's children and maintaining that perfectly manicured picture to hide the muck underneath it all.

Something was changing though, something was

reverberating in the distance like butterflies softly batting their wings. It was that subtle but observable.

Sophie was not bending her knees or nodding to show her respect to white people and she called my mother Sid. When they were little girls, Sophie went to work with her mother, who worked for Grandma, and so her and my mother struck up a friendship that not even Grandma could get between. They laughed together about everything; my mother told her about the girls at her boarding school and Sophie told her about the girls at her school in the village. Months passed when they didn't see each other and they'd be reunited during the school vacations.

—

Back then, like most women, Sophie heeded the call of taking a man's name and casually told my mother one day that she was getting married to her long-time boyfriend, Bongani. "Oh Sophie, are you sure that's what you want?" my mother responded.

"I've always loved him Sid, so yes, I'm sure this is what I want." She was radiant and crackling with excitement. My ma hugged Sophie and cried.

"I'm sorry Sophie, I shouldn't be raining on your happy parade. It's just that I can't help but worry. Some of these men lead two lives and can be two people. But I'm sure Bongani will treat you well."

My mother looked so small next to Sophie and she seemed to shrink and shrivel. Seeing her with tears in her eyes was hard to watch.

"Please Sid, don't get upset, you look like Grandma Annie and I'm sure you don't want that!" Sophie and Ma collapsed in a heap of giggles and it felt like I could breathe again. Like I had been holding my breath and my lungs were straining. Watching them without them knowing I was there made me love Sophie a little more. She always managed to squeeze breezy and happy moments into tight spots in our lives. She had a tougher constitution than my mother and, while they were the same age, my mother seemed so lost while Sophie seemed like someone constantly straining and having their leash reined in.

I always felt on edge when my father was home and Sophie was there. It felt like if I was quiet enough, I could hear Sophie hissing under her breath. She felt like a snake ready to strike when she saw my father backhand my mother. Like she was about to sink her fangs into him and fill him with venom. I used to get anxious watching them dance their deadly dance.

As fearsome as my father was, there was no doubt who would win if he ever got to the point of cornering Sophie. I knew that, unlike her mother, Sophie kowtowed to no one. In her dreams, the images she saw of herself had nothing to do with her being a servant. Her dreams were full of things that she herself couldn't believe, but she held onto them because they offered her respite and steadiness and she welcomed them without understanding them. She saw herself as free and as self-reliant with her own business rather than being somebody's maid.

My father resented the easiness between my mother and Sophie. During their courting phase he wasn't aware of their friendship and so when they got married, he had to try to tame his backhand. There were many times he had to restrain himself when Sophie was around and she and my mother giggled together. His backhand felt natural, like muscle memory.

Aside from what little my father was taught about the English when he was growing up, he was curious and fascinated by them. He thought they were delicate and sophisticated. That generalization started with his English teacher who was porcelain-skinned and gentle in everything she did. He wanted that in a wife, but at the same time he hated it because it made him feel inadequate, unsteady and oddly frightened that he would never be enough. He convinced himself that sleeping with an English rose would be a trophy for him. It would fill up the spaces within him that niggled and nagged like a woodpecker pecking at a tree. He thought it would smooth away his uncouthness and his rough-around-the-edges upbringing and turn him into a gentleman.

My mother was disgusted by the stories of how the British tortured women and children in the camps. She took it all in and felt strangely responsible and offered herself as something of a sacrificial lamb. She would try to right the wrongs of her forefathers and love an Afrikaner boy so much that it would undo the rage the Afrikaners felt for the English.

It was the same mission she dedicated herself to in attempting to close the gap between her and Sophie. She decided that that burden was also hers, that she would try to right the wrongs but ultimately she would never be able to close the color gap between them. Society was shaped in such a way that she and Sophie were friends but also employer and employee. Sophie had a life in the township that my mother knew nothing about. It frustrated her but she settled for what society allowed and she knew it was pointless to try read into it any further.

Inherited guilt is like slow poisoning that kills people like my mother. Stealthy, gnawing and counting on its anonymity, it fed on her and she visibly aged even when she was in the blooming stage of life in her thirties. I sometimes think about the moment my father laid eyes on my mother. I can almost feel the sliminess of their invisible tormentors stretching out towards each other, grabbing and entangling their tentacles to fuse and feed off each other, their demons sucking their souls until one of the parasites wins and dominates the other. They were like walking Venus flytraps luring each other into their death traps. Gruesome as this sounds, it was the primordial-infested wound that bound their relationship together. No one would admit to this kind of attraction, to this desire to engage in an invisible fight to the death.

I used to sometimes eavesdrop on my father with his army friends and what I heard woke up the sleeping beast inside me. I could tell by some of the stories that they were scandalized by what many of them had done but there was also undeniable arousal underneath it all. They spoke about one of their own moving to Thailand having fallen in love with a pretty girl who was actually a boy. Their words traveled from behind that closed door into my ear pressed against the door and warmed my whole body, settling in my rebellious loins that seemed to grow a mind of their own. The men's over-exaggerated sense of disgust planted small seeds inside me, vile things that I shut away and that grew as the years went by.

Sophie had taught me the trick of walking silently into a room by walking on the pads of my feet. I used to smell her lavender scent before she even came into a room and so I knew at that moment that she was standing behind me. She dragged me by my ear and pulled me away from the adult conversation, but I had started rebelling so while I was burning with shame, I defiantly shot her a scowl as I crept back to my room. She pointed a finger for me to go to bed and gave me a stern look, but I think she knew her days of mothering me with any sense of authority were numbered. Soon I would be coming into my own, becoming a "master," and I often wonder how many women like Sophie grieved for the babies they once loved who grew into monstrous strangers in their teenage awkwardness. The total eclipse of their humanity by the time they were adults.

It took me a while to admit to my decaying generational curse. Growing up as a white man born in the apartheid state, I had a blind and false sense of security about being in charge of people. Telling them where to stay, what their movements could be, when they could be in the city, the number of hours they could work, the amount of money they should be paid and the type of jobs they could have. You can regulate people right down to who they fuck and when, but the sticky part is when it gets to what they think. That is where our impotence is laid bare. The way they look when they think you are not looking used to send shivers down my spine. Whether it was Sophie murdering my father with her eyes or Adam the gardener shooting my father with a murderous gaze, it all left me deeply unsettled.

My father was a legend in law enforcement. He had a proverbial monkey on his back and always had things to prove. That monkey was relentless and never satisfied and was always on the lookout for signs of weakness and proving he was not quite good enough. He buried himself in his work but his demons had a way of showing up at the most inopportune time. Like when you have top-class visitors and a cockroach decides to strut down the runway of the dining-room table. Almost as if to remind him, just in case he had forgotten that he was not enough, that he was inadequate. It was a mind disease that severely tortured him.

When I became a teenager, that demon showed up with a gut-wrenching Bruce Lee kick. I was in my hiding place with Gugu as we couldn't be seen in public together. It would have meant her being branded as a sell-out for sleeping with the enemy by her people and my people branding her as a dirty stain of shame on the race and on the family. An inappropriate cockroach, who if my father had seen, would have undoubtedly caused him to lose all reasoning and unleash hurt to stamp out any imperfection to his bloodline.

I was five when I first met Gugu so she must have been four years old. I couldn't believe my eyes when Divine, the maid from next door, brought her to work. She had no one to look after her and so Gugu was part of the package if the Krugers wanted their house cleaned. Gugu was fascinating to me from the get-go; she was so brown my young mind thought she was made of chocolate. I was curious because she was small and cute and almost like a doll. Years later, she told me she was both frightened and tickled by the sight of me when she first met me. To her, I was a boy with transparent eyes and incomplete skin.

I asked her if she tasted like chocolate and she simply giggled and stared at me. She was curious about my hair. She was also puzzled by me trying to show her how far my pee could go when I was standing up, having only been around her mother and grandmother who peed sitting down. I thrust my little hips forward as if to push my pee further but she was not impressed and couldn't believe there were people who peed standing up.

I asked her again if she was made of chocolate and she replied in a language I couldn't understand, so I did the next best thing and licked her round forehead. Instead of chocolate, I tasted the salty trace of sweat as she did too, I suppose, when she mimicked my actions and licked my forehead. The damp heat of Durban leaves everyone sweaty and we giggled, gleefully unaware of the shock that my Grandma Annie felt when she witnessed our act of innocent curiosity. She had a bad hip, which made it difficult for her to walk, so she took a long time to get to us but she grabbed my arm and marched me to the bathroom.

"That little girl looks like chocolate but she tastes like salt," I said to my grandma. It was clear she was upset but I wasn't sure why.

"Joseph," she cut me off with a voice that was firmer than I had ever heard. "Listen carefully, we never ever play like that with other people. You will get very sick from their germs. Rinse your mouth out this minute!"

Her vehemence took me by surprise and I was defiant when I felt threatened, "But Grandpa kisses you all the time and he doesn't get sick." I pulled a face and folded my arms, tucking my little hands deep into my armpits. I sulked and stuck out my bottom lip and I knew I had won when she dissolved into fits of giggles watching her little prince pout with self-righteous, childish indignation. I wanted to laugh too but I fought it, making my expression even more comical.

"That is a very different kind of kissing, my lovey. What your grandpa and I do is for big people and your grandpa is not chocolate, is he?" and she wagged a finger at me. She tried to ignore the fact that she was crimson red with embarrassment.

"What you just did is not polite. You can't go up to people and lick them because you think they'll taste like chocolate. You'll thank me one day when you grow up and realize that people carry very bad diseases. And this better not reach your pa's ears; he'll be very disappointed in you." My grandma had a serious tone and I sensed she meant something deeper than my childish understanding could process but I never forgot that day.

That was the start of a secretive and beautiful friendship between me and Gugu. We'd meet in my tree house that was built in the tree that straddled the Krugers and my family's property. I would play my harmonica, which I think was far more interesting to Gugu than I was, but I tried not to compete and enjoyed every minute I spent with her.

≡

Looking back all these years later and now that I know about the Mandela effect, I know the way my father would remember how he caught us in the tree house that day would be different from mine, and most definitely different from Gugu's memory of it. The day is branded into my memory forever.

It was the mid-80s and my father disappeared for spells, dealing with intensifying riots and calls to "Free Mandela." He'd come home in a foul mood and use foul language and particularly hated some dominee, Beyers Naudé, who he called the spawn of Satan for betraying the Boers. Naudé worked hand in glove with Allan Boesak in their calls to free Mandela.

My father must have heard Gugu and I in the tree house that day as we were arguing about what we were going to do as we had just found out she was pregnant. I was trying to calm her down, kissing the birthmark on her elbow. We used to imagine what shape was most accurate to describe her birthmark; I thought it looked like a lopsided heart, while she believed it was where God rested his paintbrush when he was painting her. So she said it wasn't a shape but a splotch of paint left by God. I used to lick that patch of her skin, teasing her that it really did taste like my mother's cooking chocolate. It was our secret and something I always did to her and she was just giving in to my persistent tongue that day when my father climbed into the tree house. He was hissing when he showed his red face.

He didn't look at me, his focus was on Gugu who was shrinking away to the farthest corner of the tree house wishing she could disappear. He knelt down next to her and told her she was a "filthy little kaffir with no morals." He grabbed her by the shoulders, lifted her and slammed her against the back of the rickety tree house.

"Dad, please don't," I whimpered and he backhanded me so hard that I saw stars. He looked back at Gugu and his face was close to her ear but I could hear every bone-chilling threat he issued. His voice was unhurried, cold and frightening, and I knew he was capable of carrying out each one of his threats.

"I know everything about you. I have eyes and ears at the back of my head and I know all your family in that village. I'm capable of killing every single one of them. Now listen to me, you and your filthy mother will get out of this town and go as far away as possible. I never want to hear anything about you contacting my son, you hear me? Otherwise I will hunt you down and shoot you and that mutt you are carrying, understood?"

Gugu nodded vigorously and climbed out of the tree house without so much as a backward glance. My father spat a gob of saliva on the floor and looked at me like I was a filthy animal.

"This better never reach the ears of your mother, understood? It ends here. No son of mine is bringing home a mongrel."

I nodded while looking down at the floor. I was frightened and felt as guilty as a dog caught stealing food.

We never talked about Gugu again. If it wasn't talked

about, then it never happened. The thunder and lightning I was waiting to strike me down never came, which left me even more keen to get out of that house.

Divine and Gugu disappeared from the Krugers. I'm sure Gugu got a tongue-lashing worse than what I got because our actions had not only added an extra mouth to feed, but they had also stopped her mother's source of income.

Gugu left a note for me hidden under a brick next to the stairs of the tree house, which had an address of a butcher shop in Gugulethu in Cape Town. It was probably close to where they went into hiding and where their post was collected but I never tried to contact her. I tried to forget. I detested my father and we couldn't be in the same room; even the cats scurried away from the tension between us. My mother picked up on it but to avoid further confrontation she didn't talk to either of us. I wasn't talking to my father and, while I could see it was killing him, I didn't care.

$$\equiv$$

The nine months I spent in the army gave me a glimpse into my father's world and why he was such a hard-ass. Repression was at its peak back then and sabotage campaigns were blowing up substation transformers. It was all a bloody mess and there was no way you could come out of the sewerage smelling of roses. It was the longing for the unknown that kept me alive and I vowed that one day I would look for Gugu and find out about our baby. I never did write to her at that address but I kept it with the hope that one day I would.

When I got back from the army, I found my mother radiant and happy and my father gone. I was relieved and couldn't work out how she had made him leave without being killed. I never got to hear that story. I helped her trace his address for the serving of the divorce papers and we got on with our lives. I would be lying if I say I missed him. Our house felt alive again and I left for university with a clear conscience, knowing that my mother was safe and happy. I studied Psychology, fueled by my curiosity into the inner workings of the mind.

A few years later, I married Jo Anne Wales, an American girl from Endwell, a town in New York State. She was one of those whites flocking into South Africa at the time for an experience of a new democracy birthing while the local whites were shipping off. We were both 25 and swimming in the euphoria of living in a new rainbow country. She was more enthusiastic than me but I was living it vicariously through her.

I couldn't say for sure that Mandela taking over was altogether a good thing but I wouldn't dare admit that because then I would be one of them, the oppressors. It felt like we woke up one morning and no one was racist, everyone whispered the word "kaffir" and all of a sudden everyone had a Black friend. The spines of docile garden boys and maids suddenly straightened, like their bodies knew and felt the shift. Blacks became more present and didn't hesitate in taking pleasure in punching the lights out of any white fool who dared called them "kaffir." They were heady days; Savuka and PJ Powers became idols of the struggle even for those who use to harass them and call them "kaffirboetie." Miriam Makeba, Hugh Masekela, the Mbulis and many others came back from exile singing us to unity.

Sometimes we even forgot why we were fighting each other. Only the die-hards associated with the likes of Eugène Terre'Blanche were a reminder. When he fell off that horse, he became the ageing buffoon known for budging in the negotiations and slapping the shit out of Rajbansi. It became a comedy of a white wolf against a Bengal tiger. Roelf Meyer and Cyril Ramaphosa standing side by side made us all hopeful and proud and they were poster boys for the negotiations that were underway.

But underneath the mass jubilations the system was still working to ensure the whites had a seat at the table, to keep the bigger slice of the economic pie. Newspapers were discrediting Winnie Mandela as she was the most feared and she was pushed out of the way with scandals believed by many here and in the international community. This caused rifts among the Blacks and resulted in the end of her marriage. The narrative gained traction and was firmly secured, along with collective amnesia and massive inequalities leaving Black people blindsided. Many were bought with business shares, creating a new class of the nouveau riche, the new members and new money.

The birth of my son, Arthur, resulted in a complete overhaul of who I was and turned my life upside down. My gregarious wife, ever the radical and a lover of all things forward-thinking, wanted to be one of the first white women to give birth at Baragwanath Hospital. I'd married her for the heady and floaty feel that came with her boundless and fearless energy to stick it to the establishment and so I said, "I'm in," when she suggested it. "If we're going to make this country work we have to be all in or ship out to sheep land."

Deep down, I wanted my son to be born in a sterile and clean hospital in town with white nurses and doctors. At night I silenced my shame with sleeping pills for my chronic insomnia. The mid-90s were an intoxicating time, full of fear and hope. Darkness was settling at the bottom of all our memories, festering and undisturbed, secure in the knowledge that no one wanted to go there.

I read that from the day a baby is born they know exactly who they are but by the age of seven they start forgetting. They use clues from their parents to fill up the canvas of who they are, whittling themselves into hollow fabrications of identities cast by their seniors. This felt like a form of death, like my son was dying to his true nature and taking up a new identity that I was responsible for. I wanted to run away and not see this horrific process come into full bloom. No one except my father knew my son wasn't my first-born and for him my first child wasn't even human and was therefore nothing to be acknowledged. He made me feel like I had mistakenly shat myself or, more precisely, like I had ejaculated prematurely and shamed myself.

My mother contracted an aggressive form of pancreatic cancer and by the time she succumbed to the disease she didn't recognize anyone. But she did know her grandson was on his way before she got too ill.

Jo Anne and I relocated to Cape Town and I started having heart-stopping moments thinking I was going to bump into Gugu and my child. Deep down, my psyche was telling that me that I had a son. I looked closely at all the colored boys I passed, searching for myself. I was thirty by then so he would be a strapping fourteen-year-old teenager. My longing to know what became of him and Gugu became a preoccupation. The letters I finally wrote and sent to that butcher shop address remained unanswered. I only had Gugu's name to go by. I didn't know the name of my son, I didn't know his date of birth, I didn't even know Gugu's last name. I had nothing to go on. My nightmares were intense and in them my torturer was no longer Sophie but Gugu.

$$\equiv$$

Jo Anne and I opened a psychology practice working mostly with white middle-class men still shaking off post-traumatic stress from the Border Wars, transitioning to democracy and broken marriages. It didn't take long for both of us to start feeling bored and restless. We hit the seven-year itch in our marriage and were short with each other, sleeping with our backs touching. I feared that Jo Anne would up and leave with Arthur and go to America.

What was driving her crazy was the hypocrisy of me wanting everyone to open up about their problems while I remained silent about myself. She knew something was eating me up and I wasn't being honest with her. Shame is a poisonous thing that thrives in the dark and is mind-altering. I was convinced that Jo Anne would leave me the minute I told her that, while I had enough to eat and sleep in a warm bed every night, I have a child out there who may be starving. I expected her to judge me as harshly as I was judging myself.

We used to talk about the pervasive issue of teenage pregnancy and how it derailed so many of the kids living in the townships. I wondered why it wasn't such a thing in suburbs because teenagers were randy no matter where they lived. Jo Anne said it was because whites knew how to dig deep holes to hide anything that was unsightly while most Blacks were so indoctrinated with Christianity, they would not dare kill an unborn baby. That brought me down from my high horse. I remembered how girls would take small pills the morning after carelessness to prevent pregnancy. Some of them would disappear from school and come back the next year with some story, having given birth and given the baby up for adoption. Jo Anne is adopted. She loved her adoptive mother but couldn't stand her father and that is what prompted her to pack up and come to South Africa. She said her father never stopped referring to Blacks as "niggers."

When our son was about five years old, he used to pull my hand to go outside as soon as he heard the ice-cream truck's jingle coming down our street. One day, Jo Anne stood in our way and smiled at Arthur and said, "I've got delicious ice-cream in the freezer, we don't want the one from the truck do we, Joseph?" Arthur looked up at me for support.

"Oh," I said. "Yes, we have our favorite one in the fridge, I forgot." We lured Arthur to the kitchen and dished him up a few scoops of ice-cream. He didn't seem convinced but he was pacified by what we had in the house. Jo Anne continued to turn him off the ice-cream truck until he stopped asking. Jo Anne said she couldn't believe how long the hands of evil racism were. She said that the childhood jingle was originally published by Colombia Records in 1916 and the lyrics were mocking Black people for liking watermelon, "Nigger Love a Watermelon, Ha, Ha! Ha, Ha!" The cover of the record had a caricature of a Black man with big lips eating a piece of watermelon and those were the kinds of things she grew up with in her adoptive home. She wouldn't have her own family supporting the continuation of debasing fellow human beings. I knew that jingle as "Turkey in the Straw" but I guess it's the old story of naked Truth being too ugly to look at. Since then, the ice-cream jingle nauseated me.

Jo Anne's intense anti-racist stance was burying the secret of my first son even deeper within me. I knew her judgement would not be that I had a child at such a young age or that I had it with a Black woman; her gripe would be that my family was ashamed that the girl was Black and that I silently went along with it.

$$\equiv$$

We reinvented our practice after a few years and opened it up to working with township communities. We roped in our landscaper, TaBigboy, an indigenous healer who knew everything about the soil and plants, and he and Jo Anne bonded over their love for succulents. They would talk for hours working alongside each other in the garden. TaBigboy was a tiny man with an easy smile and he talked in riddles. He called me Sonnyboy and addressed Jo Anne by her name because we had insisted that he didn't address us as "Sir" or "Madam." TaBigboy knew a lot about medicinal herbs and ones that could help addicts drop their drug habit, an area that Jo Anne was particularly interested in. After a lot of research, she decided that we should open a short-term rehab center with prolonged aftercare integration counseling for addicts.

One day TaBigboy and I were chatting and he said, "You know Sonnyboy, you hit a jackpot with this one." We were sitting in the shade watching Jo Anne working in the garden and talking to her succulents. I nodded and smiled admiringly at my feisty-spirited wife with her large sun hat, old garden clothes and ridiculous Crocs on her feet. There comes a time in a man's life when he stops chasing skirts and realizes that he has won the jackpot and would choose his wife again and again.

Just then I felt full inside but TaBigboy continued, "But you're messing it up with all your secrets, you know that." I was so shocked I spilled my juice all over me and he cracked up laughing, "Relax my boy, what man doesn't have something to hide? You know I have lived long and seen many a moon fill up and empty. What I can tell you is this, whatever you are keeping from her will not be the undoing of you two. You have an unbreakable bond. Grow yourself a pair and face the music. You'll thank me when that boulder in your chest is gone. Shame is alive only if it is unspoken; speak it and you will be free. Good luck, Sonnyboy." He stood up and walked away, leaving me stunned.

That night Jo Anne and I conceived our daughter, Sarah, and I emptied myself of my shame and she held onto me as my tears turned into lust and we took comfort in each other's bodies. My little Sarah became a reminder of how life can be renewed and produce miracles.

A few months later, Jo Anne, who was heavily pregnant by this stage, was unfolding the newspaper looking for laptop deals and the front page of the *Cape Times* had a large picture of matriculants jovially celebrating their passes. Just below the main story was a photo of a young mother with her son who had scored As in all his subjects. He was tall and beaming at the camera and the mother was wiping tears from her face. Her elbow birthmark sent me reeling and I felt like the room was spinning.

Arthur thought I was playing a game so he started giggling but Jo Anne said I looked like I had seen a ghost. I couldn't speak and pointed at the photograph. I'd recognize that birthmark anywhere, even in my sleep. It was Gugu and it wasn't hard to work out that the boy with shaggy Afro curls and pale eyes was my son. He had the distinctive cleft chin of the Van Rooyen men. It's funny how certain things we hate about ourselves sometimes turn out to be symbolic later on. Jo Anne looked at the picture, put two and two together and her jaw dropped. She then looked at me with panic in her eyes because her waters had just broken. Our Sarah was not getting left behind on this ride.

I dashed to the bath and filled it with water and called our doula; Jo Anne was having a water birth at home this time round. We spent the rest of the day tending to Jo Anne. I was also so excited about my discovery. It was early the next morning when Sarah finally made her appearance. I had not been in the room when Arthur was born as the nurses at Baragwanath made me stand outside, despite Jo

Anne insisting I should be with her. I had told her that we had to respect the African culture where men should not see everything that goes on when a baby is born. Those nurses saved my ass because I wasn't ready to see the gory things I imagined happened during childbirth and Jo Anne had begrudgingly let it go. I winked at the nurse, who smiled a knowing smile as I sat outside and prayed it went well.

It was a different story with Sarah and I saw everything and, instead of being horrified, I gained a new respect for a woman's body. The way it carries, feeds and then expands for the life of a tiny human being to come out was a miracle. As soon as Sarah howled her lungs to greet us in this world, I stepped out the room and cried my own grateful tears for my family.

$$=$$

Jo Anne's first question the next day was whether I had contacted the newspaper. I hadn't yet as I had watched her and my new baby sleep, looking from Sarah to the photo in the newspaper. What if Gugu and my son wanted nothing to do with me? It was possible that they thought I was a racist monster who was happy to forget that they ever existed. It sat heavily in my stomach. It also hadn't even occurred to me that I could call the newsroom and ask for Gugu's contact details from the journalist who had covered the story. I felt a little stupid when Jo Anne suggested it; I sometimes hated her moments of resourceful clarity.

I searched for the newsroom's number and made the call immediately. I didn't want to lose the little chutzpah I had. I got through to the reporter but she wouldn't give me Gugu's number and said the best she could do was to ask her permission first. She promised to get back to me. I was slightly relieved because by the time I spoke to Gugu, she would have at least had a slight warning. A week later, the journalist contacted me and said Gugu didn't want to give out her contact number but requested that I give her mine. I gave her my details, including our home number and address, and she promised to pass the details on to them. Two days later I received a devastating text from Gugu:

> Dear Joseph, my son is not ready to meet you just yet. I am working on him but his Van Rooyen stubborn streak is strong. He snarled like your father when I told him that you made contact. I will do what I can, you will just have to wait this one out like I waited for your letters, Joseph. Be well.

I started to feel what Gugu must have felt like waiting for my letters all these years. Time passed and I heard nothing more from Gugu. Things were tough and Jo Anne had her hands full with a baby and Arthur, as well as encouraging me to not give up hope and reassuring me that Gugu and my son would call when they were ready. I told TaBigboy everything as he had become a bit of a father figure that I looked up to. I noticed how easy it was to unburden myself to a man who was not white like me. I felt a little freer or maybe safer because I felt like I was heard with a different filter.

=

TaBigboy was short in stature but he was a giant of a man. I watched him bring back a lot of men from the brink of being swallowed up by drugs. He would make them drink a concoction of his that made them vomit and shit and cry out their demons. The first time Jo Anne and I sat through one of his sessions he had to restrain me because I was convinced that the man was dying. TaBigboy grabbed my hand and sternly pointed for me to sit down. We sat throughout the night witnessing the agony of that man. At daybreak he knelt near the man and sang an old Khoi song and reminded the man that he was of Khoi-Khoi blood, a man among men. Jo Anne and I then worked with the man in counseling and helped him integrate back into society. He had no cravings for drugs but he felt he had no purpose in the world. TaBigboy helped him get his life back and he eventually enrolled at the Mount Nelson Hotel to do culinary studies after realizing he loved food. He told us he had seen it in his visions the day he took the concoction but it took him time to put it altogether to make sense.

"He'll call when he's ready, give him time," TaBigboy said. He said it like it was a given, which was both affirming and maddening, but I knew him enough to still hang onto hope. Jo Anne and TaBigboy warned me not to call the number and she often found me rereading the text until she took my phone and deleted the message. If I didn't know any better I would have said she was jealous, but I knew she was rescuing me from myself once again. I was a sucker for brooding in emotional turmoil. I knew the message by heart; I knew my son snarled like my father and Gugu's parting shot about her waiting for my letters didn't make it any easier.

My little Sarah was an old soul and when she started walking she'd quietly waddle over to whoever was the object of her affection. She knew when someone was feeling down and would calmly climb onto their lap and wrap her stubby little arms around their neck and hug them. When she did that to me on my hard days, I'd try not scare her with my tears. We called her "old lady" because she seemed to take charge and she would squeeze your cheeks and cover you with wet kisses.

Arthur was eight and Sarah was three when Jo Anne decided that it was best to tell them about their older brother to avoid any confusion should he one day decide to show up. She believed that Arthur was entering the stage where he was solidifying his identity and he needed to have a foundation where honesty, no matter how ugly, was the best policy. One night after supper Jo Anne told the kids that I had something important to tell them and so I told them the story of their brother who lived with his mother. Arthur thought it was the coolest thing and wanted to meet him but Sarah was too small to really understand. It went better than I thought and I suspect that certain things wait until the circle is complete before they materialize and start a new one.

It was a few days after telling my children that I got a call from Gugu. She said our son was graduating cum laude from the University of Natal where he was studying Psychology and Philosophy. I had to smile to myself at the irony of that. Gugu caught me up on all her news. She had survived the wrath of her mother, which melted and cooled when she gave birth to Joseph Junior Vusumuzi Zulu, or JJ to most of his friends. Gugu's mother forced her to go back to school and finish high school while she looked after the baby. Gugu finished school and then immediately joined an airline to become a flight attendant.

In the township she endured ridicule and teasing and got into many fights to defend her son who was ostracized and ridiculed for his pale grey eyes. He was given many nicknames like snake eyes, cat eyes, mehlomlungu—white man's eyes. When JJ became a teenager he fended off the bullies himself and the bullying soon subsided as he was tall in stature and obsessed with lifting iron. Gugu said he was a quiet, thoughtful boy who didn't give her too much trouble.

When he was fifteen, Gugu decided it was time to tell him everything about me. Instead of feeling sorry for himself, she said he hugged her and thanked her for keeping him and looking after him. When Gugu suggested that they look for me he snarled in response and refused. He did the same when Gugu told him I had seen them in the paper but he had said he wasn't ready. Gugu said she was planning to use his graduation to appeal to him again because she believed that every growing boy needs to know and be mentored by a father figure. Gugu had never had other children or got married and still laughed in the easy way she used to.

I caught her up on the bloody fights with my father after he caught us in the tree house, my time in the army and my family with Jo Anne. By the end of the long call there was an understanding that she held no grudge against me and there were no hard feelings between us.

I told Jo Anne all about Gugu and that my boy was called Joseph Junior and went by his mother's surname, Zulu. We laughed in unison at the irony of him studying Psychology. I told her that JJ was apparently a gym fanatic and a reader and, with Gugu working for an airline, they traveled extensively. I got the sense that their mother-son bond was strong and I was so relieved that he had turned out so well growing up without a father. I felt sad that I never got to see Divine to thank her for helping raise my son but she had already passed on by then. After that first call, I anxiously waited to hear from Gugu again.

I didn't have to wait too long as I received an email from JJ himself a few weeks later.

Dear Mr. Van Rooyen,

I wanted to wait until I had a plan before contacting you. I didn't want you to feel obliged to pay for anything that had to do with me. I traced you out of curiosity and I knew about your work at the rehab in Gugulethu and that's how I know TaBigboy. My mom told me what happened with you and your father. I hated you both but I was born to a woman who taught me not to hold grudges and raised by a grandmother who could raise hell but was also full of tenderness. Having your blood running through my veins has brought me a lot of suffering. I was teased and bullied but I'm not complaining. My grandmother and mother gave me a lot of love and care. They raised me to know the difference between the things I could change and the things that are just the facts of life. Like when your father forced them into hiding.

It would make my mom content if I invited you to my graduation so consider this note an invitation. I want to surprise her so if you are communicating with her please don't spoil it and tell her about this email. I will continue to fob her off when she suggests that I call you.

Please know I have no expectations of you. I plan to do my Honors and further postgraduate studies at UCT and, since my grandma passed, I've decided to move to be closer to my mom. I am not expecting you to be a father. Having studied Philosophy I suppose I chose you to be the vehicle for me to be here so you owe me nothing. So thank you, more for your sperm that outran the billion others to cause a cosmic collision with my mother's egg to give birth to me. That is how TaBigboy put it to me. Lucan, a great philosopher once said, "Some men by ancestry are only the shadow of a mighty name." I have accepted my lot as the man who interrupted the great tradition of pure-blooded Van Rooyens.

Let me know if you will be coming to the ceremony and I will secure a ticket for you. The graduation will be at the Colin Webb Hall on the Pietermaritzburg campus on April the 3rd.

Kind Regards,
JJ Zulu

JJ

LITTLE DO I know, but just like many of my Van Rooyen ancestors, I find solace in writing. Putting pen to paper and telling my story makes me who I am. Now that my graduation is finally here it's time to face my father. I am done with school without his help. I have enough leg muscle to stand on and face him man to man. After all, TaBigboy initiated me and called me a man. It will be a perfect surprise for my mother and I know she's been waiting for me to give in and meet him. My journals will come in handy for him to know how I was loved and raised by the two greatest women in my life.

Many of the boys I grew up with were raised by women so I wasn't an anomaly. I didn't grow up with any shame, but when I entered puberty I began to feel lost and angry. TaBigboy was a father figure to many of us in Gugs and helped many of us stay out of trouble. He listened to my story, often without saying a word, and sometimes I'd think he had fallen asleep. When I eventually stopped talking he'd say, "Boy, have you ever worked out who you are without this story?" When I told him I hadn't, he said, "I think it's best you find out who you are before you get swallowed whole by anger and bitterness. Otherwise you will be driven to something worse, something that will having you smelling of self-pity. That will be like having a monkey on your back that will make you hesitate to be your best self because you are a man who was abandoned. It will have you beating up women, it will have you stealing and using all forms of distraction. You will never want to take any responsibility because you were a man who was abandoned. But I'm telling you that is not your story, not if I can help it. I've seen too many good boys get swallowed whole well into their old age, walking around still feeling sorry for themselves. We better slash open that festering wound and drain it of its pus before it turns into poison." TaBigboy left me confused but with a lot to think about that day. Mostly about who I really was without the heat of anger in my chest.

≡

When I turned fifteen, TaBigboy and his son, Uncle Smallboy, took twelve of us to a camp in Sutherland. Uncle Smallboy is a tall raggedy man with dark skin and next to his short, yellow-skinned father they look unrelated. TaBigboy asked our families for permission to take us away for the weekend and our mothers and grandmothers all agreed because he had performed miracles with boys in the township over the years. Some who had been tik terrors in the community came home changed men and never touched that venom again. Some of us were just angry and aimless boys in danger of getting into bad habits; it was just a matter of time.

That weekend, TaBigboy had us build a crude shelter with bamboo. It was a small round structure not high enough for any of us to stand up in. He pointed each of us to an allocated area and told us to remember who we were seated next to because when the structure was complete it would be pitch dark inside. He dug a shallow hole in the middle of the shelter and we were all curious and wary of what was going to happen. We covered the shelter with old, thick prison-issue grey blankets and by the time we were done, the shelter looked like a dungeon. Outside, Uncle Smallboy had a raging bonfire going and there were twelve round stones smouldering red in the fire. He kept turning them over like he was cooking them. There were large buckets of drinking water and a jug placed inside the shelter. TaBigboy kept the jokes coming to try ease our growing trepidation. We ate our supper of samp and beans and afterwards we watched the sky light up with stars we had never noticed before. The night was still apart from the sound of the river below us.

TaBigboy then said, "Right, young men of Khoi-Khoi, I want you to remember we are all men among men sitting here. Every man with two balls hanging between his thighs was born to be a man among men. Whether you are Malawian, Zimbabwean or Zulu or Xhosa, the outside life force that breathed its breath on you intended for you to be

Khoi-Khoi, men among men. We are going to crawl in that hut and let that life force breathe upon us again, cleaning out our made-up stories and reminding us of the lion hearts that beat in our chests."

We stripped off our clothes and TaBigboy laughed when he saw our underpants, saying they looked like women's panties. He told us men were not meant to wear such tight underpants and that we're meant to have space and hang loose down there. He said a man's testicles should always be two percent cooler than the body's temperature and hanging loose was to preserve the sperm inside them. "These tight things will kill your babies before they are even born. If you want a family in future you need to keep your 'aartappels' loose!"

One by one we crawled into the hut, remembering the seating arrangements, only able to make out the faint outlines of one another. We all sat with our knees up and once we were all seated, TaBigboy picked up the red-hot stones from the fire using a shovel and handed the shovel over to Uncle Smallboy. He then placed the stones in the hole in the floor inside the hut. Each time he placed one in the hole he said, "Welcome Grandmother," and by the time he placed the twelfth rock we had all joined in the chorus of "Welcome Grandmother." There was a stone for each of us. TaBigboy crawled into the hut and closed the opening to the shelter with a blanket. Him and Uncle Smallboy took turns spraying water on the rocks to let off steam. The temperature in the hut was boiling and we were all sweating like we had run a marathon. Uncle Smallboy sprayed us with cold water to cool us off and that was a huge relief. He put branches of eucalyptus in the water and then touched the stones with the leaves releasing the Vicks-like vapor for us to breathe in easy and deep. He threw pine cones in the fire which also gave off a soothing smell. We sang old songs and TaBigboy chanted things that only he could understand. At around midnight, TaBigboy asked each of us to tell the grandmothers what was hurting each of us. We all took turns speaking our truth and Qiniso was the last one to speak. TaBigboy had seated us strategically.

We were all grateful for the dark because only the darkness and glowing stones witnessed our tears as Qiniso told his story. His birth father was a neighbor who refused to acknowledge him as his son. He was a church leader with a wife and other children and Qiniso had to watch those children live a life with a father who was his but who wouldn't so much as send a gift for his birthday or Christmas. What was worse was that his mother continued to worship in the church. His grandmother had told him the family secret, saying that she did not want to die carrying dirt in her chest.

Qiniso's pain as he was telling his story was so deep it first came out as a growl and then later TaBigboy took him outside as the growl turned into something primal. We heard them walk to the river and we sang and chanted in the hut with Uncle Smallboy. We finally left the shelter and ran to the river, plunging ourselves into the cold water. We sat with towels and blankets and silently watched as the red sun rose from the east. We felt lighter, scrubbed clean by the steam of the gum tree and the pine. Most of all, we felt heard by all the old women we would never know.

We slowly eased ourselves back to reality after an incredible night of purging.

$$\equiv$$

And that is where I left my self-pity. I can't say I came out knowing exactly who I was, but I came out knowing I would never use the fact that I was abandoned as an excuse for anything. The only clue I had about my new story was that I was born to be a man among men.

We returned home and continued learning from TaBigboy. He showed us how to work the soil in the community garden and it calmed us, connecting with the earth like that. He left me hanging when I asked for advice about making contact with my father when I passed matric. He laughed and said that when I was ready I would know. He also instilled in me that the world owes me nothing and I owe myself everything. TaBigboy saved me from a lot of bitterness and pushed me to chase myself at my own pace. I am a man now, I have a knowing of who I am so I can allow space to know my past without feeling swallowed by it.

JOSEPH

I TELL JO Anne about JJ's email and we sit in silence and read it together. There is no doubt that I'm going to JJ's graduation and so we buy tickets to fly to Durban and book accommodation at the Elangeni Hotel.

I drive to Pietermaritzburg alone on the day of the ceremony, my heart beating in my chest like a drum. I arrive early and sit in the parking lot for a long time, biding my time and watching as the proud parents and students file into the hall. I get out when I see Gugu, whose eyes widen with surprise when she recognizes me. I tell her that JJ contacted me when I see how shocked she is to see me and we walk into the hall together. She looks well and is as beautiful as she was when we were kids. We proudly witness our son's achievement and Gugu is in tears. I hold mine in, not wanting to be an emotional mess.

I recognize JJ from the photo in the newspaper by his

shaggy Afro. He is standing in the line next to the stage, waiting for his name to be called. He spots us both and waves while his mother takes a video of her son's special moment. I spot the birthmark on Gugu's elbow and smile to myself remembering days gone by. Afterwards, JJ squeezes his mother in a hug and gives me a firm handshake and a manly shoulder bump. Whatever discomfort I had imagined and anticipated there might be melts away.

We go for a meal together at a nearby shopping center. JJ is a cool cat. He's engaging and easy to make conversation with. He teases his mother playfully and tactfully stays away from any difficult topics or issues. He is a man coming into his own and there is no need for us to rush anything. His demeanor matches his email. He is steady and the feeling of respect between us is mutual.

Gugu and JJ agree to meet Jo Anne and the kids the next day and I drive back to the hotel feeling lighter, like I've been holding my breath for decades and I can finally exhale.

We meet for lunch in the hotel and things go well. Arthur is completely taken with JJ and Sarah climbs onto his lap and gives him one of her reassuring hugs. Jo Anne and Gugu chat easily and after lunch we walk along the promenade. Soon it's time to say goodbye, with Gugu taking a flight back to Cape Town that night and JJ heading back to campus.

We've stayed in touch and, since moving back to Cape Town, JJ has been to visit us a few times, sometimes joined by TaBigboy. TaBigboy has become the unofficial patriarch of our eclectic, chosen family. When I seek his advice about whether I should ask JJ if he might consider changing his surname to Van Rooyen, he laughs until I recoil a bit and realize my foolishness and whiteness.

"Has the boy asked to take your last name?" he asks, his eyes dancing with amusement.

"No, but ..." I don't go any further, recognizing my presumptuousness and arrogant sense of entitlement. Later on, TaBigboy explains the African tradition where a child who is born in the matriarchal home out of wedlock belongs with his mother's family with his mother's name.

"Son, don't play with the hornet's nest," TaBigboy warns me. "You have already gotten off easy. I did a lot of spadework for you as it is!" I never raise the issue with JJ but I still think JJ Vusumuzi Van Rooyen has a nice ring to it.

$$=$$

JJ is bitten by the academia bug and after completing his Master's he scores a scholarship to do his PhD at the University of California, Berkeley. His girlfriend, Zinhle Ndlela, is going to go with him. We celebrate his move with a picnic at Kirstenbosch Gardens. Arthur is a lanky, shy teenager and Sarah a precocious seven-year-old. TaBigboy is stooped over with age but he still has a warrior spirit in his eyes. Gugu is the only one for who time has stood still and she doesn't seem to have aged. I can't help notice how diverse we are, like a real modern family. Zinhle, JJ's girlfriend, is a smart and beautiful woman who bears a striking resemblance to Gugu. JJ shrugs this off when I mention it and says men end up with women who are essentially their mothers anyway. When Zinhle is around, JJ loosens up and he reveals far more of his thoughts on race matters, something he doesn't really discuss with me. It's like another layer to him that I get a glimpse of when Zinhle is there.

JJ isn't the only one taken by Zinhle. She completes her dissertation on our rehab center and the healing modalities that incorporate indigenous knowledge. Zinhle and TaBigboy grow close and I think the old man feels young when her feminine attention is on him. I tease him about it and he laughs with a wink and says that an old man is grateful for any feminine energy that reminds him of the fire that once lived inside him.

It is a sad day when we say goodbye as they leave for California. Arthur is excited that he will get to go to America to visit his big brother one day and Sarah is in a world of her own with painting and music. We watch our children grow and become their own people and continue our work with TaBigboy, dealing with lots of difficult cases at the rehab but never giving up on anyone.

Jo Anne and I watch as things change in the country and it's hard for us to see how much damage our generation, and those before us, have caused. TaBigboy helps us see that our role is to listen and that we don't need to be front and center for things to change. By being present we become better listeners and often able to decipher what is being said without it actually being said. Arthur and Sarah learn with us and we have many discussions as a family as to what decolonization means and the experience of white fragility.

When Corona hits, JJ and Zinhle fly home and I'm relieved that they decide to. I feared for the safety of my Black son in America where police brutality against Black bodies is becoming a sport. While JJ may not carry my last name, I share the same feelings that Black parents do for their children.

We watch as the world is turned upside down. Toilet paper becomes the most sought-after commodity. Curfews like during the apartheid days become a thing again, even for us whites. The tables are turned as we stay indoors and wild animals begin to pop up on the empty streets of the city. The smog clears but we can't enjoy the fresh air. Rivers clear and fish come back from exile forced by our dirty habits that pollute their water. TaBigboy says it is the Creator's way of cleaning up all the years of the unnatural order of things in the world.

My world is thrown into even more chaos when I receive an email one day. It yanks me back to the past with such force that I am left reeling. It's from a Zoe Zondi, a nurse at De Groenkloof Old Age Home.

Dear Mr. Van Rooyen,

My name is Zoe Zondi and I am a night nurse who looks after a man I believe is your father, Mr. Hans van Rooyen. I have found some papers indicating that you are his son. He is not in good shape. Sometimes he calls for you in his sleep. He has told me about all the pain he caused you and your mother. He doesn't have long and I think you both may find some peace if he could talk to you one last time.

Please contact me and I will arrange the necessary paperwork with Ms. Rajah, the head of the old-age home.

Kind Regards,
Zoe Zondi

MADALA

SOMETHING IS UP with Zoe. She is preoccupied on that laptop of hers. I've stopped watching the news as it's getting stranger by the hour. There's a nervous energy and I'm feeling more tired every day. I am sad at the thought that my Girlie will be leaving me soon but at the last minute she decides to extend her contract a little longer.

I drift in and out of sleep, waking up with her keeping watch over me. Sometimes I feel so confused that I think she is Kristina. I wake one morning to find her standing next to my bed with two men. It takes me a while to recognize my son.

I get out of bed slowly and stand up, supported by my walker, shaking like a leaf. My Girlie leaves us but I want her to stay. I am grateful for the diapers I have to wear because I feel my bladder give in.

Joseph is a middle-aged man, his hair peppered with

grey. We can't shake hands or hug because of this damn virus and our chairs are arranged on either side of a table. I feel like a deer caught in headlights.

I weep openly as my son tells me how Zoe tracked him down. He tells me that the man with him is his son. He sees the confusion on my face and reminds me of that day all those years ago in the tree house. The horror of recollection on my face makes them both shift uncomfortably and I babble apologies. My son pushes a photo album to the center of the table but I'm shaking so much I can't reach for it. I must be a pathetic sight.

The young man stands up as tall as a giant and comes closer. Gently paging through the album, he tells me about my other grandchildren, Arthur and Sarah, his half-brother and half-sister. Soon we are all laughing, with my grandson calling me "Ou Timer." He has an easy way of relating, just like my Girlie does, and puts me at ease despite what he knows I did to his mother. I see my son wipe his tears and he moves closer. I look in amazement at both of them, seeing how the fruits of my loins have expanded. There in that sunroom we sit as three generations of Van Rooyen men. Sons of Kristina and Oumagrootjie and Sidney and Gugu.

Zoe walks in with a cake and I realize it is my 81st birthday. I blow the candle out, my heart so expanded and full. I now know pure love and the naked Truth has not killed me yet.

ACKNOWLEDGMENTS

To the strange old man who told me stories of war while laughing and crying at the same time, thank you. I didn't know then that it was memory making that would spark a story. After sitting in the shadows of the usual doubts, three warrior women came with such gentle kindness I could cry. They helped me push through by affirming the story I so loved creating. My sincere thanks to publishers Andrea Nattrass and Sibongile Machika, and to editor Jane Bowman. Jane, I truly appreciated your magic guidance and polite prodding. Sifiso Moshoetsi, thank you for taking the time to read the roughest draft. In fact, you have read all the un-pretty drafts of my books. Kwande. Umuntu umuntu ngabantu.

$$=$$

In the process of writing this novel, I consulted some interesting and useful resources, including:

Christi Carras. 13 August 2020. "The ice cream truck song has a racist past. So Wu-Tang Clan's RZA wrote a new one," *LA Times*.

"Jean-Léon Gérôme Artworks," via The Art Story (https://www.theartstory.org/artist/gerome-jean-leon/artworks/).

JEH Grobler. 2004. *The War Reporter: The Anglo-Boer War through the Eyes of the Burghers*. Cape Town: Jonathan Ball.

FAMILY TREE

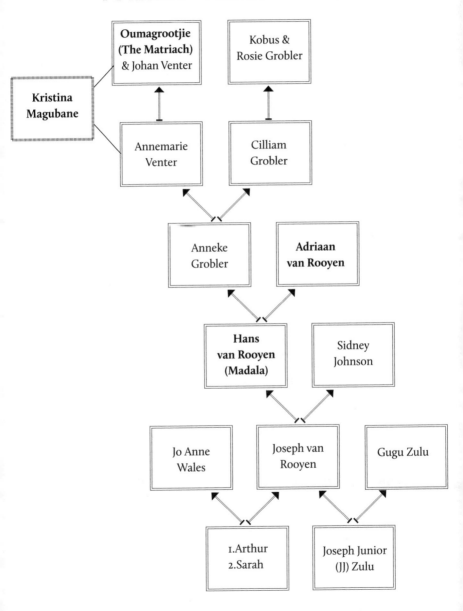

GLOSSARY

Bangbroek (Afrikaans, slang): Coward.

Boer (Afrikaans): Farmer; this term was used to describe settlers of Dutch, German and French Huguenot descent in Southern Africa from the 17th century. It has also come to mean a conservative white Afrikaans person.

Gemmer: South African ginger beer.

Gogo (Zulu): Grandmothe.r

Groot Baas (Afrikaans): Big boss.

Ja, nee (Afrikaans, slang): Literally meaning "yes, no," this expression is used to express agreement.

Kaffir: An offensive ethnic slur referencing Black people in South Africa.

Klein Baas (Afrikaans): Young boss.

Laatlammetjie (Afrikaans): Late lamb, often used to describe a child born late in the parents' relationship.

Lobola (Zulu): Bride price.

Look-up: (Afrikaans, slang) Someone who is goofy.

Madala: (Zulu) Old man.

Malkop: (Afrikaans) Hothead.

Ma se kind: (Afrikaans) Mother's child.

Meisiekind: (Afrikaans) young girl, child of my mother.

Meneer: A title of address equivalent to sir or Mr.

Mense: (Afrikaans) People.

Mfana: (Zulu) Boy.

Mkhulu: (Zulu) Grandfather.

Mvelingqangi: (Zulu) God.

Oke: (Afrikaans, slang) Dude, guy.

Oros: A brand of concentrated orange drink in South Africa.

Oumagrootjie: (Afrikaans): Great-grandmother.

Padkos (Afrikaans): Snacks and provisions for a journey.

Swaer (Afrikaans): Brother-in-law.

Tommies: Slang for a British soldier.

ALSO BY FUTHI NTSHINGILA

Do Not Go Gentle (2014)
"Urgent and sensitive, Futhi Ntshingila's writing bluntly plunges us into the brutal reality of her heroine, Mvelo."
—Gladys Marivate, *Le Monde*

"The simplicity of the language employed distills the novel down to the values that are at its center—those of love, family, and friendship." —Danielle Faye Tran, *Africa in Words*

Shameless (2008)
"It's a compelling read, a true South African story which we should all read." —Papa Molakeng, *Sowetan*

"Ntshingila's *Shameless* is full of surprises. The twists and turns gripped me to devour it in just four hours. I could easily relate to the lives of young Thandiwe and her friend (Zonke) in rural KZN—the games, the chores, the little fights." —Dr Lulu Gwagwa